"True Friends of the Heart," continutes the adventures of the main characters in my first book, "The White Starched Apron."

Maggie, Red and Glenda Faye go their separate ways, but this book brings them back together once more.

There are all new adventures, trials and tribulations to over come. There is love, sorrow and much happiness when, "The Fearsome Three Some, continue their lives during World War II, in Speedway City, Indiana.

True Friends of the Heart

Saragene Stamm Adkins

iUniverse, Inc.
New York   Bloomington

True Friends of the Heart

iUniverse books may be ordered through booksellers or by contacting:

iUniverse
1663 Liberty Drive
Bloomington, IN 47403
www.iuniverse.com
1-800-Authors (1-800-288-4677)

Because of the dynamic nature of the Internet, any Web addresses or links contained in this book may have changed since publication and may no longer be valid. The views expressed in this work are solely those of the author and do not necessarily reflect the views of the publisher, and the publisher hereby disclaims any responsibility for them.

ISBN: 978-1-4502-7388-6 (sc)
ISBN: 978-1-4502-7390-9 (dj)
ISBN: 978-1-4502-7389-3 (ebk)

Printed in the United States of America

iUniverse rev. date: 11/15/2010

Dedication

This is the sequel to my first book , "The White Starched Apron." This book continues the adventures of my three main characters, Clara Margaret, "Maggie," Mann, Sandra Kay, "Red," Murphy and Glenda Faye Kelly.

This book like the other one is dedicated to my family, without their help in supporting me and urging me on with the publishing aspect of my writing, these books could not have come to fruition. I also want to thank the rest of my friends who loved me and had faith that I could write and finish my books.

I am returning to God for the second time, to ask for His help in writing this book and hopefully, giving me the time to finish it. I dedicate this book to, "The true readers of my heart." The wonderful people who have purchased my books and come back for more of the adventures of my three girls.

Saragene Stamm Adkins
aka/ "Maggie"

FOREWORD

I started writing this book over a year ago, it is the sequel to my last book, "The White Starched Apron." I wrote a few chapters and stopped, I just didn't have it in me to write another novel.

I went back to making what I call, "My Big Comfy Blankets, after almost a year and approximately 100 blankets later, I tired of this too. I was tired and bored, I did not know what to do with the rest of my life. I was given a year to live in 2007, due to lung cancer, I chose no treatment. I came home to die or start dying to live, I chose the latter.

My daughter, Lariann, was worried about me, she thought I was giving up and maybe there was more truth to that remark than I care to admit. She nudged, pushed and hounded me to go back to the book I had started. Finally I came upstairs, turned on my computer and clicked on my book.

There waiting patiently in my word document, were my three main characters, Maggie, Red and Glenda Faye. All they needed was for me to call them back to life. They wanted to tell their stories to all the, "Readers of My Heart."

This has not been an easy task, there were days when my pain was so intense, that I could not get out of bed. Lariann would call me everyday to see if I was writing, when I told her no, it was not a good day, she would say, "Tomorrow will be better." She usually was right, I loved Maggie, Red and Glenda Faye, I did not want to die and leave their stories untold.

This book is a simple story of love, integrity and friendship. It is a quick read, but there are so many lessons to be learned from reading it. Please, don't pick the grammar apart, I did not have it edited. My time is unknown and I wanted to get the manuscript to the publisher as soon as possible. This is for my readers, but mostly for my daughter who was interested and helped me every step of the way. Without Lariann's help there would be no, "True Friends of the Heart." Thank you to everyone who stood behind me and I cannot leave out my real life friend, Glenda Faye Kelly. My other two character based friends, have passed on, I miss them everyday. One was my mother, Clara Margaret Mann and the other was Sandra Kay Harless.

Chapter 1

"Maggie will not let go!"

Maggie was sitting in her big soft chair in the living room, she was thinking about the heart-warming visit with her two best friends. Her friends were taking their afternoon nap. The three of them had been inseparable for their whole lives. Maggie's granddaughters had arranged a surprise visit for the three women, a few months after they had all celebrated their 90th birthdays.

Maggie knew this had not been an easy feat; the two women were frail and had to have a competent companion to accompany them on their flight. The girls had them picked up in a limousine that drove them to Maggie's house. Maggie's granddaughter's, Patti Cay and Lariann, kept in constant contact with their families by email every day they were here in Speedway City with Maggie.

After the shock of seeing her two friends, Sandra Kay, "Red, Murphy and Glenda Faye Kelly, things returned to normal in the old Mann residence. The women talked none stop about their young years, each one speaking of their wonderful husbands. They had to stop and remember the triple wedding that took place on a cold Christmas Eve afternoon in 1941. They had all

1

changed their last names at the same time; even in marriage they could not be separated.

Clara Margaret, "Maggie, Mann, had married, Leo John Van Camp, nicknamed, "Ace." Sandra Kay, "Red," Murphy, had married, John Ryan after giving up her vows as a missionary nun in the South Pacific. Glenda Faye Kelly married Josh Wakefield. It sounds like something out of a fairytale, but this was not true, their young years were an up hill struggle in one way or the other. One thread that kept them together was the thread of life, love and friendship from one heart to the other.

Lariann and Patti Cay, cared for the three women with the tenderness they deserved, they had heard so many stories about these sister's of the heart. Now they finally got the privilege of meeting them in person. They cooked for them, when they would let them in the kitchen, but they always sat with them drinking tea in Maggie's mother's kitchen. They loved this kitchen where so many decisions concerning their lives had been discussed and solved. They never failed to insist on drinking their tea from the little china teacups with the hand painted violets and intertwining green stems and leaves.

The Great Aunts, Lena, Beana and Rose had made the whole tea service, hand painted with violets and stems with green leaves. Due to a disastrous cat accident, only two cups and saucers remained intact. These cups and saucers were over 100 years old. Now, with the addition of the cup and saucer Lariann and her late mother, Saragene, had found in an antique shop before she died, there was a set of three. Remembering Maggie's daughter's passing brought tears to her eyes. Her two best friends had been too ill to make the trip for Saragene's funeral service.

Red and Glenda Faye could lighten the mood and bring the subject back to the Great Aunts or something pleasant. They did not want Maggie dwelling on sad happenings, due to her age and physical problems. They remembered these special spinster sisters, they were milliners and wig makers. It was never a party, unless the Great Aunts were there, especially on New Years Eve.

They looked so cute in their paper hats all in different colors, they loved to blow on the little paper whistles that would roll out and snap back.

Each night Lariann would help the three ladies prepare for bed, she was surprised when they insisted on sleeping together in Maggie's old iron bed. She knew the ticking of the old wooden clock on the other side of the wall would comfort them. As if they were young girls again, giggling themselves off to sleep. Who was Lariann to say where they could or could not sleep? The nights were still a little cold, so Lariann went to the closet and brought down one of her mother, Saragene's, big comfy blankets and placed it over the women.

Lariann stood for a moment looking at the three ladies, lying side-by-side, and holding hands. Their eyes were closing as she switched off the overhead light. She wondered what dreams would come to them, would they be of the old days? Lariann whispered, "Sweet Dreams, true friends of my heart."

Lariann went to her Grammie Maggie's spare room, undressed and cuddled under another of her mother, Saragene's, big comfy blankets. As she drifted off to sleep she tried to imagine the old frail women in the next room as young vibrant women. Lariann floated off to sleep, dreaming of the stories the ladies had related to her each day over the last week of their stay.

Chapter 2

"The Wedding Ceremony, Christmas Eve 1941"

The priest officiating at the triple wedding, at St. John's Church, had just pronounced the three couples husbands and wives. He said, "Gentlemen you may now kiss your brides." They kissed each other in a fashionable way, in front of all the guests in attendance. The girls dropped their husband's hands and stepped in front of them, they joined hands, raised their arms and said, "We Are, The Three Sister's of St. Ann's, True Friends of the Heart!"

The audience, who knew these remarkable young women, stood up and cheered and clapped till their hands hurt. It was so like the three of them to pull a stunt like this, their husbands looked at each other, they had no idea what they were in for!

The three couples marched down the aisle one after the other, the girls giggling and speaking in a manner that only they understood. The grooms once again just looked at one another, smiling, knowing all three had the only women they would ever need for the rest of their lives.

The immediate families of the three couples followed behind to be whisked off to the reception party. Everyone climbed into the waiting automobiles, the snow was starting to fall in huge flakes, the kind you can see a perfect design before it melts away. This was perfect, snow for Christmas. The bridal party was escorted together, in the same big black sedan, rented for the occasion. There was champagne and crystal for toasting a special occasion in a beautiful rosewood compartment built into the side of the sedan. It was so pretty that Maggie reached out to touch the velvet side panels and rub the soft material with her hand. "Look at this, do you believe three small girls that grew up in little Speedway City, are now riding in such luxury?" Red, being the jokester, said, "I cannot see what you are talking about, I have my eyes closed, I am afraid to open them, fearing this is all a dream."

Glenda Faye was silent; this was a bittersweet moment for her, right after the wedding, Mr. McAtee, her former father-in-law, said he had something to tell her after the reception. Glenda Faye wished Mr. McAtee had kept silent and at least given her this night with no worries. She would not let this ruin her wedding night. "I loved our wedding, it was perfect, each one of us a bride in our own right, but yet all together as one," said Glenda Faye. "Yes, I will remember this for the rest of my life, the only thing that could compare to it, was the day you came up out of the lake and I saw you for the first time," said Josh Wakefield, Glenda's new husband. Glenda Faye, turned bright red, she remembered that hot summer day, when she threw caution to the wind, giving her swimming suit a toss up to the beach. Josh, was standing on the beach when she came up from a little dive in the water, all she could see was his wonderful smile with teeth as white as the snow that was falling all around them now. "Yes, that was really an embarrassing moment at the time, but after I got my clothes on, the rest was history, as they say. I knew at my first glance of you, that I was falling in love, as we sat and talked as the sun was setting over the water. When you had to leave me there alone I thought my heart would break," said Glenda Faye.

"Enough of the sadness, this is our party, let it begin right now, everyone grab a glass, I will pour the champagne," said Ace,

Maggie's new husband. Everyone held up his or her crystal goblet and Ace poured a hefty amount of bubbling amber liquid for the toast. The bottle was empty when he finished and they all knew to take it slow, they had a whole night before them to drink and party at the reception.

Red held up her goblet and said, "For the first time in my life, I have no words of wisdom for the three of us, make that, the six of us. All that comes to mind is happiness, loyalty and love, with those three attributes, you cannot go wrong in life." "For having no words, you sure picked the prefect toast to our futures, I think that just about covers everything, we just have to abide by our own rules, just set in place by Red," said Maggie.

"I would like to make a toast, I will keep it short, here is to Patricia, who I know was with us this night, watching over the small baby named after her," said John, who is Sandra Kay's (Red's), new husband.

John Ryan had been married before, but his wife, Patricia had lost her pregnancy in a partial stillbirth, on a cold snowy night such as this very night. Patricia never recovered from the ordeal and passed away, as some would say with a broken heart. When Red rescued a small infant from the jungle in the South Pacific, just before the Japanese took over the island, she met John Ryan. They fell in love and adopted the little boy. In Patricia's honor they named the infant Patrick Joseph Ryan, also for Red's father, Joseph Murphy. Everyone in the sedan had tear-filled eyes, but they were happy tears for Mr. and Mrs. John Ryan.

CHAPTER 3

"Maggie Has Questions"

Maggie leaned back against the soft velvet of the seat in the sedan, she looked at all three of the grooms, and she wondered what kind of husbands they would make. She put her own father up as an example to live up to, he was kind, gentle and fair, and the traits you look for in a man. There was one time Maggie remembered when she questioned her father about the relationship he had with her mother.

The time in question was in late August, she and her daddy were gathering the last of the summer harvest from the garden. "Daddy, Maggie said, I want to ask you something, but I am fearful of the asking of such a personal question." Daddy looked at Maggie, with a puzzlement on his face. He said, "Go in the house and fetch a salt shaker and come meet me at the arbor bench. We will talk this out over some fresh ripe sun kissed tomatoes."

Maggie did as she was told, she returned to the garden bench just as daddy was finishing washing the tomatoes under the garden pump. She had brought out a bowl and two napkins along with the salt shaker. Daddy seated himself along side Maggie,

"Now what is this monumental question you have for me?" asked daddy.

Maggie took a gulp of air and kind of choked, the words were hard coming, but she thought to herself, "Here goes nothing!" "Daddy, I am going to get married and I want to know how you have kept your own marriage on such an even keel for so many years? I have been there, and for as long as I can remember, mother has had really blue periods and would snap your head off for absolutely nothing. You would always put your arms around her and say, "Now, now, mother, everything will be alright." It always happened in January and February of the year, what brought this on? How did you cope with her for so many years," said Maggie.

Daddy laid down his half eaten tomato, wiped the juice from his chin and said, "Maggie, my dear child, there are things that happen between a husband and wife that only they can share and bare together. That is why when these distant memories come to mind, they can only take it out on you, because only you understand their hurt."

"I don't understand," said Maggie. Daddy went on with his story, it was the winter of the worse diphtheria outbreak that anyone could recall for many years. Your mother had nursed me through a light case of it, but it still was a three month ordeal. I was sick from Thanksgiving until after Christmas of that year. It was before you or your youngest brother, Joseph were born. We lived on the east side of Indianapolis at this time, there was your mother, your first brother, little Harold and baby James. Mother was pregnant again with her third child at the time.

We were having a fierce snow storm when I got home from working on several large estates going up on the east side of town. Myself and Austin Bates were making the cabinets and the beautiful woodwork on the inside of the mansions, because of the winter weather. Mother was at the stove, she was humming an old Irish tune, Harold was only six, but he was a big help to your mother, he laid out the table and kept your brother James occupied. James was banging his spoon on the wooden tray of his high chair and making blubbering sounds. He was such a happy little toddler as was little Harold, as we came to call him. He would always say, "I am a big boy, papa."

Mother put supper on the table, she had made Harold's favorite potato soup and hot buttered yeast rolls. I don't know how she did all she did, with being pregnant and two boys to care for. There was peach cobbler still bubbling on the back of the stove. We said grace and started to eat, Harold wasn't eating, he stirred his soup, but didn't eat but a teaspoon or two when he laid his spoon down and put his head in his hands.

I got up and went around the table, I looked at your mother and said, "This little one is burning with fever!" Mother immediately came to feel Harold's head, she had such fear come over her face, I thought she was going to faint. I picked the little boy up and placed him on the cot beside mother's sewing machine, where he would take his naps while she sewed. While mother took care of Harold, I cleaned the kitchen and tended to the baby. I was in the living room parlor when mother came in, she was white as a sheet. She said, "You have to go to the chemist and phone the doctor, I believe it is the diphtheria and I don't know what to do for a small child."

I did not waste any time, I bundled up to fight the cold for the mile long walk to the chemist shop. The snow was blinding and it took twice as long to make the trip. I stamped my feet and talked to the chemist and he called the doctor for me, they talked and he related my dilemma to the doctor. I was given three bottles of medicine and instructions for the administration to little Harold. I thanked the chemist and made the long trip home against the snow, when I walked in, I was half frozen, I put the medicine against my chest to keep it from freezing on the walk home.

Mother was bathing little Harold with a basin of cold water and propped him up on pillows so he could breath easier. I undressed and came in with the bottles, my hands were so cold I almost dropped them, but mother came to the rescue and caught my hands in hers. We really did not exchange many words about our fears, but we both knew it was a grave situation. I told mother exactly what the chemist's instructions were, which were the same as the way she treated my illness a few months ago.

I sat by the stove, the baby was asleep in his crib in the front of the house. Mother heated the outing flannel with hot water that had the camphor oil poured into it. This would help Harold breath easier, she kept cold compresses on his little forehead. Harold looked up at us fussing over him and said, "I am a big boy, papa and momma, and you don't have to make so much of my headache." Mother couldn't take this, she turned away and went to the stove and cried silent tears for her beloved little boy, her first born. He had slipped so easy into this world, not a whimper and causing his mother little discomfort. She prayed to God, I could hear a few of her words and they were the same as mine, "Don't take our little boy!"

I told mother after Harold drifted off to sleep that we were to take the baby away in the morning according to the doctor. She knew she could depend on her best friend, Mrs. Murphy, without even a phone call. Mother sat up in her rocker all night and dosed fitfully as did Harold. I slept with the baby, I knew I had a long day ahead of me tomorrow. The snow had stopped and the wind had died down, thank the good Lord for this favor.

The next morning, when Austin Bates came to pick me up for work, I filled him in on what had to be done due to Harold's illness. Mother bundled the baby up till you could not see his little face, Austin carried his little valise to the horse drawn truck and I carried the baby. We got inside and drove the horses as fast as we could to the Murphy's house. The day broke with warm sunshine and no snow, we pulled up in front of the Murphy's, I got out and Austin handed me the baby and the valise.

Mrs. Murphy answered the door and pulled me inside and shut the door against the cold. I handed her the baby and told her what was taking place at our house with little Harold. She broke into tears and she unwrapped the baby. As soon as she saw those big brown eyes looking out at her from the baby blanket she couldn't help but smile. Mrs. Murphy told me not to worry about anything, she had everything she needed to care for James. She had miscarried two babies already and she was prepared with both pregnancies, but her nursery was complete except for a little one to fill it.

I returned to the truck and Austin and I went to use a telephone, I called the doctor and he was going to make a stop at our home and told me not to worry. I felt better and confident that he would be there with mother and little Harold. I climbed back into the old wooden truck that had, "Bates and Mann Cabinet Makers," painted on the side. We then headed back to the east side and worked the rest of the day.

The sun was going down when Austin dropped me off, the doctor's horse and carriage was in front of the house. I had a chill go up my spine, it was not from the cold, and I did not want to enter my own home. The doctor was at the door to greet me. He did not have to say anything to me, I tossed my cap and coat on the floor and ran to the kitchen, mother was sitting in her rocker, and she was rocking little Harold and crying. I took my son from her arms and held him to my chest, I would never see those big Irish blue eyes, so like his mother's, again.

I fell to my knees, still holding our little boy, the doctor came over and tries to take him from me, but I would not let go. Finally mother knelt down beside me and put her arms around the both of us and we cried out our grief together.

We buried our little Harold at Holy Cross cemetery on a cold blustery winter day, such a small coffin. I remember thinking, my boy was, "A big boy, papa."

Daddy came back to the present, he said, "Now you know why your mother is blue, sad and snaps at us during these two months of the year. She will never get over the loss of her only blue eyed child, who slipped away from this world as easy as he entered it. Only she and I can share this hurt together, I love her more in January and February than any other months of the year.

11

I know she is going through her hurt as if it was yesterday, but she still cannot talk about it to any one.

Maggie laid her head in her daddy's lap and cried for the brother she never knew and for her mother who had picked just the right man to marry. A man who could share her hurt and her happiness equally. She only hoped her choice of a husband could be half as good as her mother's.

CHAPTER 4

"ON TO THE RECEPTION"

Maggie came out of her reverie and back to the present, she realized everyone was laughing and having the best of times and she had been in the past for what seemed an eternity. Red was calling her name, "Maggie, hey, Maggie where are you?" Maggie smiled and apologized for her mental absence, I was just sizing up our new grooms and comparing them to our fathers. Red and Glenda Faye laughed out loud and Glenda Faye said, "That is not fair, we only know half of the story on our fathers and we have yet to know the story on our own choices of husbands." Leave it to Glenda Faye to come up with a wise exit from what could have been an awkward situation.

The snow has stopped falling, all was silent, as the big black sedan pulled up to the reception hall. The grooms helped each one of their brides out of the sedan surprising them by sweeping them off their feet and carrying them into the foyer of the hall. Everyone was already there, the girls stopped at the restroom to relieve themselves and freshen up before making their grand entrance.

When the three couples walked into the hall, everyone was already in full swing, the band started playing the wedding march again as each girl found their own father. Staying with tradition, each bride danced the first dance with her father, then he would hand her off to her new husband. Mrs. Murphy, Kelly and Mann, all had to reach for their handkerchiefs to catch the tears falling down their cheeks.

Just as the dance was ending little Patrick Joseph let his presence be known with a loud howl. He saw his new mother and father dancing around the floor. They came by and picked him up and finished the dance with him in their arms.

When the dance ended, the brides went to the family table together and their new husbands went with the brides father's to be introduced to family and friends. Of course, there was also a small amount of liquor flowing between the men in attendance. After all, almost 95% of the crowd was Irish in one way or the other and everyone knows they like to take a nip or two on special occasions!

The fathers of the brides sought out their wives and they all danced to an old Irish ballad that was tradition from hundreds of years ago back in the old country. Each mother looked at their daughter, they thought they were each beautiful in their own right, but together their beauty was something only God could make.

Mrs. Murphy looked at Sandra Kay, or Red, as she was called by her friends and thought of the trial she had been through. Such a tiny young woman, standing only five feet tall, her dress was overwhelming her, it was the same dress she had worn when she took her vows to become a bride of Christ. The thought of this small young girl running through a jungle with an infant tied to her body, was almost unbelievable, but true. Mrs. Murphy saw John Ryan in the crowd and wondered what would have happened if he had not pulled the mud soaked little woman onto the airplane about to take off from that island in the Pacific. Sandra giving up her vows was hard to deal with, but Mrs. Murphy knew that

God always had a plan and this was His plan. Sandra Kay was sparkling, sitting between her two best friends, her red hair was growing out and she reminded you of a little red headed pixy with bright green eyes.

Mrs. Murphy was not the only mother admiring her daughter, Mrs. Mann was in wonder when she watched Maggie holding little Patrick Joseph. She thought to herself, I wish that I was a grandmother too, but that would have to wait for her. Maggie's dark brown curls framed her face and showed off her huge brown eyes, so like her father's. Sadie Mann loved her only daughter more than life its self, they were very close, no secretes only trust and honesty between them from the start. Philip, Sadie's, husband held her a little closer and whispered in her ear, "You are still my bride, your beauty is as radiant as the day we danced at our own wedding." She just smiled and a blush came over her face.

Mr. and Mrs. Kelly waltzed by the table, Glenda Faye blew them a big kiss and turned back to her conversation at the table. Mrs. Kelly thought back to the days when Glenda Faye was small and there were eight little Kelly's running around their family home on the outskirts of Speedway City. How hard, this now grown woman worked and helped raise her siblings. Her first marriage ended in an annulment and broke her heart. The family of her first husband, Scottie McAtee, had taken very good care of Glenda Faye and she now wanted for nothing. Thank God for sending Josh Wakefield to that little strip of beach on a Summer day when Glenda Faye was at a very low point in her life. Today she shined, her long auburn hair hung to her waist and she had flowers entwined in the braids holding the sides of her hair back. Fairy princess, came to mind for Mrs. Kelly, she was such a tall skinny little girl that bosomed into a magnificent lady. Mr. Kelly hugged his wife, just glad that she was still here with him and to see her daughter get married to a man she truly loved. He almost lost her to a female cancer, but thanks to Maggie seeing the signs of her problem, her life was saved.

The dance ended and everyone gathered around for photos and the cutting of the cakes. Mrs. Minerva Bates had made the cakes, she made every cake for every special occasion the girls had celebrated. There were three cakes each with a tiny bride and groom, but one cake also had a tiny baby attached and laying in the brides arms. There were many toasts and cheers as the brides and grooms stuffed cake in one another's mouths, thank the good Lord that the cakes were white. Red had smeared cake all over John's mouth and chin, she just could not help being a jokester when ever she had the chance.

The Great Aunts were sitting at the family table, tonight they wore brand new hats and dresses made just for this wedding. Maggie walked over and brought each lady a piece of cake to eat and one to put under their pillows for good luck as was the Irish tradition. They all laughed, they knew they would not follow the tradition and wish for a husband like so many young women would this night. Maggie loved her aunts, Leana, Beana and Rose Kelly. They had made her wedding dress and veil, allowing her mother to help, but only under their guidance. The ladies thanked Maggie for remembering they loved the little whistles that Maggie had laid out just for them. She did stop at the funny paper hats, but the Great Aunts wore hats of their own making and for the first time in the fashion of the day. Normally they would have been large hat with many flowers and ribbons or feathers. Maggie knew they worked very hard on their outfits, she had many photos taken with the Great Aunts that night. She never wanted to forget them, she wanted to stop them in time and cherish their love for her forever.

Red stood up and walked across the room to her mother, Mrs. Murphy was sitting with Sadie Mann and Mary Kelly. She leaned down and told her mother that little Patrick Joseph needed a diaper change, they all laughed out loud. It did not take long to realize what needed to be done, the three of them took the little baby to the women's lounge to diaper and change Patrick Joseph's outfit. Sadie asked Mrs. Murphy if she could speak of something very personal? Irene said, "Since when have we ever had anything personal enough that we could not discuss it?" Sadie took a breath and then she said, "Patrick Joseph does not have the features of the island natives in the Pacific, his color is so light and his hair curls like the softest down. His eyes are large and round, an amber with green flecks, not the black color of the natives." Irene smiled at Sadie, she said, "I have spoken to Sandra Kay and John about this very subject. They both agree the baby's father was probably one of the airmen sent to build the air strip on the island. The mother was of course as Sandra Kay knew, was a native who left the small infant at the mission." Mary Kelly agreed with the other two women that he was an unusually beautiful baby, the mixture of cultures gave him the best they both had to offer. One day he would fit right in with the world he now was blessed to be in.

The reception went on for hours, no one wanted to leave, it was the biggest event in the history of Speedway City, and the whole town had been invited. Close to the end of the reception, Glenda Faye's ex-father-in-law drew her aside, Glenda's heart went to her throat. What could he have to tell her at this very moment when all was going so well? Mr. McAtee said he did not know where to start, but just came out with it. His son, Scottie, Glenda's first husband, had been killed in a bombing in one of Britain's hospitals. He had enlisted in the service and gone overseas so help in any way he could, being a doctor, and there were so few to be had in the war. Glenda could not help the tears that started streaming down her face, Mr. McAtee held her tight and dabbed her tears and calmed her down. He said, "I would not have told you this, but in my wife's will she left Scottie's inheritance to his children if he was to remarry, but he did not. The inheritance was then to pass to you, Glenda. You are now a very rich woman, I know the circumstances are dire in the receiving of it, but that is just the way it is." Glenda told Mr. McAtee that she would put the money to good use since she already had enough from Angela's will when she passed away. Glenda kissed the older man and hugged him, he turned and walked away towards the front of the reception hall. She could tell he was a broken man who had lost his beloved wife, Angela all to soon and now his first born son.

Finally the wedding party announced that they were going to take their leave and begin their three day honeymoon at a very elegant hotel in downtown Indianapolis. This treat was provided by Ace's mother, she had rented the three rooms for the wedding party. With the president declaring war on Japan just a few short weeks ago, there was no time for a formal honeymoon to Europe or the Hawaiian Islands. The couples had things that needed to be done, the wedding was so quickly planned and executed that there were a lot of loose ends to be tied up.

Everyone threw rice, blew kisses and photos were snapped as the six young people exited the hall for the waiting sedan that had brought them to the reception. The snow had started again but the night was beautiful with a full moon shinning down between the clouds. The couples were tired to the bone, but so happy and excited to be starting their lives together. Glenda Faye sat back and thought about Maggie and Red, she knew first had they were both still virgins. Even with having been married before, Glenda Faye had saved herself for Josh Wakefield on this happy night. She wanted to be as close to a virgin as she could for him. Her first marriage was not a pleasant experience, so she did not know what to expect from Josh. She just knew when he held her and kissed her she melted like warm chocolate in his arms.

The sedan pulled up in front of the hotel, there were several people on staff to greet them and make them welcome. This was all do to Ace's mother's instruction beforehand, she had planned everything down to the last detail. Bouquets of flowers in every room, a bottle of champagne and wonderful Dutch chocolates with cherry centers. There was bubble bath and lovely French soaps in the private bathrooms. She had purchased big fluffy bathrobes for the brides and grooms, which were spread out on the beds along with flower petals. She left nothing to chance, their luggage had been delivered, unpacked and put in the appropriate place.

She had purchased imported nightgowns and matching slippers for each of the brides that hung waiting in each dressing room off of the bedroom suites. Now all that was needed was the wedding party to open the doors and begin their lives as married couples.

CHAPTER 5

"THE HONEYMOON"

The newly built hotel was opulent, the three couples stared around trying to take it all in. This was state of the art décor for 1941, for one thing, they had never seen so many telephones in one place, they were every where. The bellman explained to them when asked about the telephones, that many of them were in house telephones, they were for personnel to use and room service orders to be delivered.

They were all silent as they rode the elevator to the penthouse suites, when they got off of the elevator their feet sank into the carpet. The bellman led them to the first room to be entered, the girls joined hands and jumped up and down and started to giggle. Josh, John and Ace were scratching their heads at this point and so was the bellman. The girls explained that this feeling was just like the time they had all met in the hall at St. Ann's School of Nursing dormitory. They stood in front of this door and repeated the same action, they were so excited as the bellman turned the knob on the suite. He explained that each suite was exactly the same and he would take each couple to their suite. The girls told him they would take the keys and he could leave them to fend for themselves. As he was leaving he informed them there was a swimming pool on the lower level for their use if they so desired. Ace already knew this and they had all packed their swimming suits.

As they entered each room the girls giggled and marveled at the pink imported marble bathtub and there was a dressing room attached to the bathroom. When Red saw the beautiful nightgown and slippers, her face turned beet red. Red had not given a thought to what was to come later that night with her new husband, John.

Red said, "Let us all make a toast of our own to each other before we go for a midnight swim to relax." The others agreed, Maggie said, "I would like to toast the two young women who have been my best friends since before I can remember. We went through school and nurses training together and started our careers at St. Ann's Hospital. It was not always easy, but we made it through. When Red and Glenda Faye left me alone in Speedway City, I thought I would not be able to go one without them, but with the help of God, I succeeded. I hope we can now go on with our nursing, or whatever we decide to do with our lives together again. I love you all and now that includes your husbands and mine." Everyone clapped, Maggie always had just the right words to complete the moment. Red lifted her glass to everyone and said, "Becoming a missionary nun in the South Pacific was not what I thought it would be, I was totally unprepared and too young for such an obligation. The good thing that came out of it all was my finding little Patrick Joseph and meeting my husband John. The circumstances were dire and I thought my life was coming to an end in the jungle that morning as the sun was rising over the airstrip. So, here is to John and Maggie's husband, Ace, who was the pilot of the airplane who flew us to freedom." Glenda Faye lifted her glass, she said, "There was a time when the three of us shared four years together in a tiny room at St. Ann's School of Nursing, we shared so many tears and laughter. We came through it with flying colors and went on to the rest of our lives. I have never forgiven myself for having to leave Maggie behind, but we all have to grow up and sometimes have to leave our childhood friends along the way. Thank God for that summer day on the beach when I met my husband to be, Josh, he is the love of my life as are my two best friends.

Glenda Faye went to find her purse and came back with a rolled up piece of paper tied with a ribbon, she handed it to Red and John. She said, "This is for little Patrick Joseph and his mother and father from his Aunt Glenda Faye." Red and John unrolled the paper, it was the deed to their new home, paid for in full by Glenda. They tried to give it back, but Glenda would not here of it, she said, "I came into my money by sad means, but I will do good with it in the future, and you are my first people to receive a gift of my love and devotion." The tears started flowing and Red hugged Glenda Faye, she whispered her love for her in her ear. Glenda Faye smiled, she was so happy with the result of her gift.

Ace, Maggie's husband, lifted his glass and said, "Now, young ladies do you think we could all change and go for that swim without anymore tears of sadness or joy?" They all laughed and went to their separate rooms, they met in the hall dressed in the big fluffy robes and slippers with their bathing suits underneath. They rode the elevator down to the lower level, there in front of them was a magnificent swimming pool. It was all done to resemble a Roman bath, with pillars and marble statues, there was even a steam room. The men headed for the steam room, they wanted to sweat out some of the liquor they had consumed and then join the girls for a dip in the pool.

Maggie, Red and Glenda Faye dove into the pool, the water was cool, but felt so refreshing after the long evening of dancing and being with so many people. They stood and then floated on their backs talking about the old days. Red said, "Remember when you two thought because I was an only child that I was rich?" Maggie and Glenda Faye shook their heads in a yes motion, "Well, Red said to Maggie and Glenda Faye, you two are the rich ones and John and I are the poor relation." Maggie and Glenda stood up, they had angry expressions on their faces, Red did not expect this reaction, she was only kidding. Maggie spoke, "Don't ever say something like that, what is ours is yours, never think any different!" Glenda Faye said, "If you have a need, just come to me, no questions asked, I will be your fairy godmother from now on. Don't let John's pride come in the way. I bet Josh and Ace are telling John the very same thing right now in one way or the other." Red felt just awful having even said what she did in jest, being her normal joking self. Red said, "Sorry, I will accept your help with love, but you know I am hard working and so is John, we want to try to make it on our own, but the house mortgage is sure a burden off of our minds. Thank you again for everything."

Splash, the three men had snuck up from behind and jumped in the pool, there were screams at the feeling of the cold water hitting them after the steam room. Everyone played around and then dressed and went to their rooms, at the door, they bid each other a goodnight and happy beginnings.

CHAPTER 6

"EXPLORING DOWNTOWN INDIANAPOLIS"

The morning after the wedding the weather had taken a turn for the better, the sun was shinning and the snow had stopped during the night. The three couples consummated their weddings, the men knew that the three girls would come together and discuss the happenings of losing their virginity.

They all met in the restaurant for breakfast, there were a lot of red faces and each girl burst out in laughter when they looked at each other. Maggie, being her bold self said, "Lets get this over with, I will go first, my wedding night was like something out of a romance novel and that is all I have to say about my sex life at the moment." Red said, "If I had known how wonderful being married could be, I would have married John in Hawaii and not waited to come home. He is a great lover, I hope I am not getting too graphic." She saw John blush and shake his head. Glenda Faye said, "I guess it is my turn, being married before seems like a bad nightmare, but my wedding night with Josh was a beautiful dream. I hope we keep dreaming for many, many more nights to come."

"Here, here," said the three grooms as they lifted their orange juice to the girls. This was a real treat, fresh orange juice in the middle of winter, it was better than the champagne in their rooms. They sat and made plans for the day, Maggie said, "I believe I would like to spend the first day with Ace all alone, that is if you don't mind?" Red agreed and so did Glenda Faye, they had not had a single moment alone for many days and nights. They finished their breakfast and gave hugs of good-bye and planned to meet for supper.

Maggie took Ace's arm, she looked up at him and said, "Would you mind spending the day in bed with me, we could order room service and make love until supper time?" Ace looked at his timid bride with surprise, but he was all for her plan and told her so. Little did they know, but the other two couples had similar plans of their own. By supper there were three huge silver trays sitting outside the door of each suite. When they met for supper there was much laughter and bright red faces, when would they get past this?

The three couples had a big supper with steak and lobster flown in from Maine. The girls had never had lobster before, when Red speared her lobster, it slipped off the platter and went sliding across the floor. The waiter being so prim and proper came to the rescue and told her he would bring another in just a few moments. They were laughing so hard, there was food flying out of their mouths, but they did not care what the other guests thought, they were so happy with each other's company. Maggie took a careful bite of her lobster after dipping it in the butter/lemon sauce, "Wow", she said, this is the best thing I have ever tasted. Well, maybe it compares with the wonderful fish served at the St. Christopher's Festival, which was Maggie's favorite.

When supper was finished, they all went for a walk around downtown and took in the latest movie. There was no popcorn for this group, they were stuffed from the huge supper at the hotel.

They slowly walked back to the hotel and went to their rooms. Maggie thought as she slipped into a new nightgown her mother had made for her, I like this being married to Ace and then she thought of her own mother and father. She ran her hand down and over her belly, maybe God had planted a seed on her wedding night and she too would know Red's joy of having a baby of her own.

The next two days seemed to fly by, there was not a department store or museum in the area that they did not visit. The girls had lived so close, but never ventured very far away from the dime stores and the L. S. Ayres department store. Glenda Faye had fond memories of this department store, if it had not been for the owner, Mr. Ayers helping out, she would never have had the money for her uniform to start nursing school. He also brought Mrs. Van Camp on to the scene, she ended up being Maggie's mother-in-law. Isn't it odd how God has a plan and it all comes together just right!

Everyone was packed up and waiting for the taxi to take each couple to their new homes to start their lives together as, "Married folks," to quote Maggie's mother. Red wondered what she had been thinking when she dressed, she had on peek toe pumps and the snow was freezing her feet. Glenda Faye of course was the practical one and had remembered to pack her rubber slip on boots. Maggie had on a new pair of gabardine slacks and tie up oxfords, she was sporting the latest fashion, and not too many women were wearing slacks as they were called, for women. Maggie loved them, when she was young, her mother cut down her brother's knickers and made Maggie a pair of her own to play in. Her brothers used to chase Maggie around and around the big tree in the back yard and she would climb up so high that they could not reach her. This could not have been done without the help of her new knickers.

Maggie and Ace were living at the Van Camp mansion on the outskirts of Indianapolis. They had the whole west wing to themselves and there was a staff of servants at their beck and call.

Maggie was bored, she wanted her own home, like her mother had. A home for her children to be raised in and come to with their own children one day. Ace had bought her a brand new car to replace, "The Old Independence," the car Red's father had given her when they were teenagers. It had been what some people referred to as a rust bucket, but it ran like a champion racehorse and never let them down. Maggie would make the long drive everyday to St. Ann's Hospital, where she was an OBGYN nurse. She loved working with the new arrivals and caring for the mothers and their babies. She still carried pink and blue ribbons in her apron pocket to tie up their hair after cleaning them up when they were delivered of their baby. Blue for the boys and pink for the girls, a little lip rouge and a ribbon in their hair made the mothers feel pretty when their husbands came to see them.

One evening Maggie told Ace that she wanted to move closer to Speedway City and her family. She said the drive was taking too much time away from their private time together and she wanted to have supper waiting for him, just as her mother had taught her. Ace understood that Maggie was not used to his kind of life, she was a simple girl with big dreams and he would do his best to make her dreams come true. Ace told Maggie to start looking for a lot to build on or to find a home she liked near her mother and her two best friends. Maggie reached over and kissed her husband goodnight and smiled, she loved him more at that moment than she thought possible.

Red and John had settled into their new home next door to her parents big stone home on 15th Street in Speedway City. Red and John were now in charge of the green grocery, Mr. Murphy had semi-retired and Mrs. Murphy took care of the baby. John loved working in the store, he had a way with people and an infections laugh that no woman could resist. Red did not let this bother her, she knew John's love was for her and her alone. Red did think to herself, will I be feather dusting cans and bottles for the rest of my life, just as I did when I was a young girl? Both John and Red noticed that their orders for certain foods were coming in short, they soon found this was due to the war. Mr. Murphy said, "You watch, it will not be long till we have rationing." He was right, this was right around the corner and coming like a speeding bullet.

Glenda and Josh moved into a new home not far from her mother's big house. It was a comfortable home with five bedrooms and three bathrooms, Glenda wanted to fill the home with many children just as her mother had. Maybe not eight, but three or four would do to start with, Josh did not care, and he knew his wife would be a perfect mother to his children. Josh was working in his father's manufacturing plant in Indianapolis, his father was based out of Dayton, Ohio, but had many plants in various parts of the country. He and Ace were considering buying a small airport on the far Westside of Indianapolis to transport the products he made for the war effort. Ace was a well equipped and a knowledgeable pilot, if he could fly Red and John out of the jungle, he could fly anywhere.

Everyone had a plan and they were coming together, Maggie was getting ready to move back to her hometown with the help of her mother. They got together and picked out fabric and furniture for her new home. Mother thought it a little too large for her comfort, but it was not for her to say. Maggie loved the big two story brick home on 16th Street, that was just about where Speedway City ended and the cornfields began in 1942.

CHAPTER 6

"THE WAR EFFORT"

Maggie was visiting her father, Philip, at the lumberyard where he worked with Austin Bates, they had long given up their cabinet company for good paying steady jobs. Maggie loved the smell of the burning wood in the big pot belly stove, the iron glue pot sitting close to keep the glue liquid for making the woodwork in the mill. Cedar hung heavy. in the air as always, if you closed your eyes you could picture the huge cedar trees in the forest. "Daddy, Maggie said, would you make the new cabinets I want in my butler pantry off the kitchen. You did a wonderful job of making my kitchen cabinets and china cupboard with my wedding crystal enclosed there now." Daddy looked up over his, Specs, as he called his glasses and smiled at his daughter, where did the years go, he thought to himself? "Of course I will, I only have one more job that has to be done by the end of the month for the Army. They need a lot of pre-built tent frames to be shipped to different Army bases, in fact, Ace and Josh are flying them out in their cargo planes." Maggie told him any time he had would be fine, there was absolutely no hurry, and after all she didn't even have a butler! They got a big laugh out of this, as did Austin Bates who was chewing tobacco and spitting it into a big can filled with sawdust. Poor Austin, he did not have one tooth in his head, just like his wife, Minerva. They were the perfect couple, nicer people could not be found in this whole world.

Maggie left the lumberyard and went to visit with Red and John at the green grocery, they always stayed open late on Thursday nights. Maggie had an idea, she had talked it over with Glenda Faye before presenting the plan to John and Red. John was in the back with Mr. Murphy, Red was checking out a customer, the store was empty now. Red was so happy to see her friend, she gave Maggie a big hug like she had not seen her in months. It was just last Sunday at mass, they all attended St. Christopher's church in Speedway City. "Red, Maggie said, Glenda Faye and I have an idea, but it will not work without the help of you and John, are you interested?" "Yes, of course, anything we can do to help the two of you." Maggie went on to tell Red that it was really to help her and John along with the whole town. Maggie said, "What do you think of expanding your store and buying the two adjoining buildings to have a Dry Goods store? You know everyone has to either drive or take the trolley to get downtown Indianapolis for fabric, dry goods and ready made garments. We could have dry goods on one side and ready made merchandise on the other. I would like to talk to the Great Aunts and have their input on what to buy, you know they have been in the business for over fifty years in one fashion or the other." Red was silent for a few moments, she then said, "I think it is one of the best ideas you two have ever had, but the money, we do not have the money." "Don't worry about the money, you will be an investment in our futures and the profits will go into a trust for the children that are surely to come. You and the Murphy's will have a hefty salary to live in great comfort, but the work will not be easy" Red ran and got John and her father, she relayed the plan to the two men, John was beaming, he knew business was weak right now and they were barely paying the bills and living expenses. "I like the idea, but it has to be a corporate organization, we will not take charity." Red thought to herself about how Glenda Faye must have felt those many years ago being a charity student in high school and nurses training at St. Ann's. How the tables turn, now here is her husband repeating almost the same words to Maggie.

Mr. Murphy was smiling, he reached out with his large bony hands and drew Maggie close to him and hugged her. "What would we all do without our three wonderful daughters to care for us, you always have been there in our time of need." Maggie started to cry, but wiped away the tears of happiness, she couldn't wait to tell Glenda Faye the good news. Glenda was attending a meeting of the board at St. Elizabeth's Home for Unwed Mothers. This was an institution where the young girls would go and wait for their due time to deliver their babies and then give them up for adoption. Glenda was also an OBGYN nurse and she had taken this institution on as her greatest charity. She was purposing a new wing and major updating to the buildings and hiring more competent staffing. Glenda came from a family of ten counting her parents and children were dear to her heart. She wanted a large family just like her mother and she could afford this.

As John and Red were walking home the weather was breaking from winter to early Spring, the cool air felt good on their faces. Arm in arm they walked and talked and made plans. It seemed with every step a new idea popped into Red and John's head. They were so excited to share their joy with Mrs. Murphy and little Patrick Joseph, even though he was too little to understand yet. He would just love the attention and laugh and giggle when held by his parents at the dinner table.

There was a time when Sandra Kay went overseas as a missionary nun that Mrs. Murphy went into a world of her own making. She did not know or care who was present in her life. All she did was sit and knit baby clothes, the needles clacking constantly, Mr. Murphy even had to take her to the store to keep an eye on her. When ever someone would as why she was knitting baby clothes, she would just look up and smile and say

"Sandra Kay is bringing home her baby and I must be ready." Sure enough Sandra Kay came home from the Philippine Islands with a baby boy, after Mrs. Murphy took the baby in her arms, the world was set to right again for her. Now sitting here at the large family table, she was feeding little Patrick bites of roast chicken and roasted potatoes, his favorite. When she heard the news she clapped her hands and smiled, "I can help you, I know all about knitting supplies and baby clothing, the good Lord knows I bought enough in my day."

So far everyone was on board for the new expansion, Glenda Faye would be thrilled, she had her own work to do, Maggie was head nurse on the maternity ward at St. Ann's and now Red and John would have the largest store in town. It would be three stores in one, you would be able to walk from one store to the other without going outside in the cold or hot weather. All was good in Speedway City this night in early spring of 1942, they had celebrated the New Year as usual with the Great Aunts and their paper hats. The men drank home brew and Irish whiskey in the basement away from their wives. The time was passing so quickly for everyone, Ace and Josh had all the business they could handle with the war effort and transporting almost anything you could think of by air freight.

CHAPTER 7

"THE WAR COMES TO SPEEDWAY CITY"

As Maggie, Red and Glenda Faye walked down Main Street of Speedway City, arm in arm, just like when they were young girls, they noticed there were American banners, flags and posters everywhere. In the houses that they had passed there were so many flags with one, two or even three stars on them. Each star meant there was a young man in one of the armed forces here and abroad. Maggie's mother and Glenda Faye's mother both had flags with stars. Maggie's youngest brother was in Georgia and three of the Kelly boys were scattered here and overseas in the Pacific Islands. How the town had changed in just a few short months, the picture of Uncle Sam was in most store windows saying, "America Needs You," with a pointing finger starring straight at you. It was a little creepy as far as the girls were concerned, but that was just their opinion.

They stopped in the drugstore for a soda, each girl had her favorite, Maggie's was strawberry, but today it did not sound good to her. She ordered chocolate, Red and Glenda Faye looked at her with question in their eyes. Maggie always had strawberry, Glenda

Faye started laughing, she nudged Red, "I think someone has a little stranger on board," said Glenda Faye. Maggie turned bright red, could that be possible, with everything that was going on she hadn't paid attention to her monthly periods. "Good Lord, said Maggie, do you really think I could be pregnant already?" Red looked at Maggie and said, "We Irish Catholics are known for our ability to bring forth many children and grow a nation." They all laughed so hard that ice cream shot out of Glenda's nose, just like when she was a young girl, she wiped the ice cream from her nose and kept laughing at Red's comment. Maggie thought to herself, here I am a nurse and I don't even know I am pregnant, wait till Ace hears the news. Mrs. Van Camp will be beyond herself having a grandchild and my mother will throw the biggest baby shower in the town of Speedway City. Wow, she thought, watch what you wish for, God has a plan.

Maggie swore her friends to secrecy, they were not even to tell their husbands. Maggie wanted to see her friend and colleague, Dr. Lucas Anthony, who was head of the OBGYN department at St. Ann's. She could have Dr. Jacob Adams, who was a partner with Dr. Anthony, but Maggie did not feel comfortable with Dr. Adams. Every nurse on the ward was enthralled with Dr. Adams, he was tall, dark and handsome, his eyes were obsidian in color. Like looking into dark black pools, you could lose yourself in his eyes and smile with deep dimples on both sides of his cheeks. That was it, Maggie would pick Dr. Anthony, he was all business and she had learned everything she knew from him.

Dr. Lucas Anthony had been called to the charity ward that cold winter night that John Ryan had brought his wife Patricia in with a still born child. Maggie would never forget that night, the poor girl was half frozen and the child was dead on arrival, having been partially born. Maggie later went to the lavatory and cried as she was throwing up, the sight was so overwhelming and unforgettable. Maggie was glad that Red had not been privy to the scene that night, how John stood it, she would never know.

Maggie tried to erase the memory and get back to the present, Ace, would be beside himself. Maggie knew he would want a son, but she did not care one way or the other, as long as the baby was born safe and sound.

The girls went their separate ways from the drug store, Red went back to the green grocery and Maggie went to her mothers house. Glenda Faye had a meeting at St. Elizabeth's Home for Unwed Mothers. She sat on the board and they were going over the plans today for the new wing that would be dedicated to her own mother who had raised eight children.

There were only three Kelly children still at home, Glenda Faye loved each and everyone of her siblings, but Sharon, Beverly and little Paul were favored by her. Paul was also Mrs. Mann's favorite, she always brought him lollypops and cookies fresh from her oven. Mrs. Kelly loved her new home with the running water and beautiful bathrooms. She often thought of those days in the past, scrubbing other people's laundry out in the side yard of her home. The little Kelly's fetching water from the pump and putting it to boil over the outdoor stove fueled by wood. Now she had her own washing machine with automatic rollers and a wash stand to hold the rinse water where to laundry would fall from the rollers. Mrs. Kelly really enjoyed doing the laundry now, it was fun for her and the other children. I guess calling Sharon and Beverly children was not right, they were in their teens and little Paul was not far behind.

Mr. Kelly was still working at the General Motors plant, but now he was head of maintenance and no longer a janitor. He would often walk over to the lumberyard and eat his lunch with Mr. Mann and Austin Bates. These three men were best of friends and Mr. Kelly remembered how they helped build the first indoor bathroom in the old farm house the Kelly's used to live in. It seemed that every bite of food consumed in the lumberyard office had a bit of saw dust in it, but that never mattered to these, "Tough Old Birds," as Minerva Bates called them.

Glenda Faye was getting ready to leave St. Elizabeth's, when she was called to the office for a phone call. She walked down the hall wondering who would be calling her at work? Glenda took the receiver and said, "This is Mrs. Wakefield, how may I help you?" There was a bit of silence on the other end of the line, then Glenda heard a squeaking sobbing noise. "Hello," Glenda said again, and finally she heard the voice of her younger sister, Sharon. "What is it Sharon, has something happened to mother?" "No," said Sharon, "It is my problem and I need to speak to you at once, I am in big trouble, please come to the old farm where we can speak freely, promise me, please!" Glenda promised Sharon and hung up the telephone, she was puzzled, what could her sweet younger sister have done that she was so upset about and wanted total privacy? They would meet when Glenda finished with her appointment at her doctor's office. She had her normal check up a few weeks ago and he had called her back for some test results.

When Glenda walked out of Dr. Whitcomb's office, she was white as a sheet, she could hardly start her automobile. She just sat there going over the results of her tests, Dr. Whitcomb had informed her that she would more than likely not be able to bare children. For Glenda Faye, this was like a punch in the stomach, she looked down at her body, so perfect, but barren. How would she tell Josh and her two best friends, one with a baby and the other already pregnant. Glenda turned the motor off and laid her head on the steering wheel and cried, deep racking sobs.

CHAPTER 8

"GOD HAS A PLAN"

Glenda Faye pulled into the drive-way of the old homestead, she saw Sharon's bicycle next to the front porch. Sharon was sitting on an old wooden chair with her head in her hands crying. Glenda composed herself and got out of her automobile, she walked up to Sharon and put her arms around her little sister. "Now, now, what kind of problem could an 18 year old girl have and kind of laughed?" "Don't laugh, this is very serious," said Sharon. "Let me tell you and then you will see for yourself." Sharon started by telling Glenda Faye the story of her young boyfriend Shawn McGill, his parents had been notified that he was killed in the South Pacific. Glenda was not laughing now, she understood exactly what her little sister was going through. "I am so sorry, Sharon, I had no idea that you and Shawn were serious about one another." Sharon pulled a gold chain from inside her dress and there hung a small gold band with a tiny diamond. "Yes, we were serious, but he said we would not marry until he returned and I was to keep this engagement a secrete." Sharon went on to tell Glenda Faye that there were far greater problems, the young girl looked up at her older sister and said, "I believe I am pregnant, I missed my monthly this month. "I know I am a bad girl, but when Shawn left, we made love the night before and now just a few weeks later this happens." "I know what to do, said Glenda, we will only tell mother and daddy the truth and I will need to share this with Maggie and Red." "Everyone will keep your secrete, we all love and care about you, now listen very carefully."

Glenda Faye told Sharon that she would come to St. Elizabeth's to await the birth of her baby and then stay a few more months. The story would be that Sharon went East to study for secretarial training and would return the following year. Glenda Faye and Josh would adopt the baby, this way the child would remain in the family, but until the right time not know his real mother, she would be his or her aunt. Sharon was relieved and knew her sister would have the right answer, she did not want to lose her child to strangers.

Glenda now said to Sharon, "I too have a problem, I found out just today that I may never have children. You know I wanted a whole house full, just like mother and I am devastated by the news. It is funny how God works in our lives, your bad news is my good news. We will share in the caring of your child for the rest of our lives, you have the right to tell that you are the real parent or not." Sharon looked her sister in the eye and said, "This is your child, God sent this child to you, not me, and I will carry it for you and Josh. You have my promise on the Holy Mother of Christ, one day, I will have children of my own when the time is right. Now I have to take care of business and grieve for my lost love that will never see his child."

Glenda put the bicycle in the trunk of her automobile and drove Sharon home. The two women walked in together, mother Kelly was in the kitchen where she always was, "Hello girls, what are you two up to, I can tell it is serious by the look on your faces?" The girls set out the tea cups, put the kettle on to boil and sat down with their mother. When the story was told, mother Kelly was in tears, but she was still happy that she would have her first grandchild by what ever means God saw fit. She would miss her young daughter dreadfully, but Glenda assured her she would bring her to see Sharon at St. Elizabeth's and arrange for her to be there for the birth.

When you live in a small town like Speedway City, you have to be so careful of what you say and who you say it to. These were times when an unmarried girl having a baby out of wedlock was to most a mortal sin against God. Thank God, Sharon, had modern women to surround her and care for her and the child she was carrying.

Mother Kelly was also upset when Glenda Faye told her about being barren, she knew her wonderful daughter did not deserve this fate. She was so caring and giving and should have had her house full of children. God did a good thing by giving her this child, even if it was not her full blood. No one who would find out the truth later would feel any different than mother Kelly did.

Maggie had just gotten home from her shift at the hospital when she saw Glenda Faye and Red's automobiles in her driveway. Her heart skipped a beat, what if Ace and Josh had been in an airplane crash, or one of her family was hurt, she had a brother in the service. Her mind was racing as she entered the house, the girls were in the kitchen drinking a coke when Maggie came running in. She slid up to the cabinet with a bang, she had been running so fast. "What is going on, what has happened, why are you here, tell me?" "Calm down, Maggie, said Glenda Fay, you are pregnant, and you might injure yourself. Sit down, I will get you something to drink, we have a story to tell you and there are many parts to it."

After the news was related to Maggie, she was so sad for her best friend, but happy too. She had known Sharon since she was practically a toddler and felt sadness for her loss of Shawn and now the loss of her baby. Maggie knew the baby would have the best mother a child could ask for in Glenda Faye and Josh would be a wonderful father. Wow, thought Maggie, here we are myself and my best friends, all with babies in the same year. Each of us has a story to tell about how we got the children, but some parts will remain sealed for histories sake concerning Glenda Faye's child.

Maggie, Red and Glenda Faye all told their husbands the news and swore them on their God, not to ever mention the details. Josh was sorry for Sharon, but he was walking on cloud nine and wanted to start on the nursery details immediately. He was so excited and glad he could share the adoption plans with Ace and John. They would all have babies by their first anniversary next Christmas Eve. What an Irish Christmas that will be, the Great Aunts will be so excited, their will be children again in the Mann household, where they held the party every year. Maybe that might have to be moved to the VanCamp mansion this year, if Mrs. Mann would approve. She always said, "My home has expandable walls, it will hold many loved ones."

Maggie and Ace had Red and John over for dinner, they too discussed the dilemma and they all thought Glenda Faye had handled it in the best and most fair way possible. So like Glenda to know just what to do or say, her feet were firmly planted on the ground and they had deep loving roots.

CHAPTER 9

"THE BUILDING BEGINS"

Spring was just around the corner, it was warming early this year, you could already see tiny buds on the flowering trees. Everyone was gathered at the green grocers for a meeting, the discussion was on the layout of the two adjoining buildings. One building had been a beauty parlor and the other had laid vacant for many years. It was full of barrels filled with straw and glass globes for oil lamps, old leather harness straps and other such outdated materials. John and Red wanted to fill one building with dry goods such as bolts of material, sewing implements and the latest sewing machines. Mrs. Murphy wanted a whole section stocked with knitting needles, yarn and patterns. Mrs. Mann and the Great Aunts wanted a specialty department with imported ribbons, lace and yard goods that you could only purchase in New York.

The men let them know that the cost would be great and they still had another store to furnish. Glenda and Maggie's husbands took on the burden of the loans, they were both rich in their own right. Mrs. Kelly chimed in, which was unusual for her, she said,

"My children grew up with homemade clothing handed down from one to the other, I would like to see ready made clothing in the new store. Work clothes and suits for the men and pretty dresses for the women and little girls. Play clothes, shirts and knickers for the young boys. There could be a section in the back for the unmentionables, meaning underwear of all kinds." " Maggie laughed, she said, I agree, but buy some pretty satin tap pants and chemises for the women, not those ugly cotton one piece union suits with the flap in the back. If we are going to do this let us get it right in the first place, we will have people coming in from all parts of the county to shop here." Mr. Murphy put in his two cents worth, "After shopping they could then come in and buy their groceries before returning home, we could call it, "The One Stop Shop." Everyone agreed with the name, it said it all.

Remodeling began the next week, there was a lot of business going to the lumberyard and the plumbing company. This would be one of the first stores to have an inside bathroom for men and women. Something unheard of in 1942, most establishments still had outside toilets that were not spoken about. Red and John spent morning to late in the evening working side by side, Mrs. Murphy would bring little Patrick Murphy by when she brought everyone a picnic lunch. He was a jolly baby, so beautiful, sitting up now and playing with little animals Mr. Mann and Austin Bates had made for him from cedar wood. He even had a little wagon to pull his animals around in, which was always upside down.

Maggie had seen Dr. Lucas Anthony, her baby was due the last week in September. She never stopped thinking of Sharon living at St. Elizabeth's, she remembered the day everyone of her friends saw her off at the train station leaving for New York City. In reality, she got off in Ohio, where Glenda picked her up and returned her to Indianapolis to wait the birth of her new baby. Sharon's baby would be due in late November, just in time for the holidays to begin.

Glenda Faye was amazed at how well Sharon adapted to her life at St. Elizabeth's, she loved working in the laundry and fixing the many meals served to the mothers waiting on their own babies to be born. There were times when there were as few as three women there and then maybe there would be fifteen all at once. Some stayed a long time others came and went after their 10 day recuperation period. Sharon's favorite time was holding the babies, so like her little brother Paul used to be. There was not one minute she thought of this as her baby, she always referred to the baby as Glenda Faye's child. The papers for adoption were already drawn up and signed by all the parties involved. Mrs. Kelly dropped by from time to time to bring Sharon little treats or a new maternity smocks and pretty nightgowns, just little things to brighten her spirits. Little did she know that Sharon was not blue or feeling bad, she was happy to be able to help out her older sister who was so happy about being a mother.

The new wing on St. Elizabeth's was in full swing, the weather was perfect, the Spring thaw was in progress and the ground breaking took place a week ago. Here again, The Speedway Lumber Company was given a good contract to fulfill. Mr. Piper, a friend of Mr. Mann's, was a good plumber and got the contract for the new stores and the hospital wing at St. Elizabeth's. With all the war contracts, it seemed everyone was very busy, even General Motor's had started hiring some women with so many men enlisting in the war.

Maggie was so busy at the hospital, it seemed that there was a baby boom since so many men had gone off to war. The waiting room was fill with pregnant women waiting for their monthly visits. Dr. Lucas Anthony and Dr. Jacob Adams, had their hands full, literally. Maggie was experiencing a bit of morning sickness, she did not like this one bit, but her mother told her to eat crackers and drink plain tea. It did not work for Maggie, but she did not tell her mother, for fear of hurting her feelings. Each time Maggie assisted with a birth, she winced a little, she never thought of it before, but now she stared her future right in the face. It did not bother her to say she was scared and did not look forward to all the labor pain. She thought of her mother giving birth to four children, all at home with just the doctor to basically be there to catch the baby and sign the birth certificate. At least here at the hospital they now had ether and gas they could give you to ease your pain or put you out completely if necessary.

When Maggie dragged in at 7:00PM, Ace was there with supper on the stove, Maggie kicked off her white shoes and headed for the bedroom. She stopped and kissed her husband and changed into her robe and washed her face and hands. Ace had scrambled eggs, bacon, toast and jam for supper, he knew this was a craving of Maggie's lately and he was not a good cook. They ate and then cuddled up on the couch and listened to the news on the radio, the news from the South Pacific was not good and the war in Europe was even worse. They decided to turn off the radio and turn in for the night, Maggie snuggled up to Ace and kissed him with so much passion, he said, "Lady, it is a good thing you are pregnant because after tonight you would be." They both laughed and turned out the light.

Red and John dragged themselves into pick up little Patrick from her mother's, Red could barely lift him from his crib, and he was fast asleep. Mrs. Murphy said, "Let him sleep over, you come over for breakfast when you get up and he will be happy to see you at the table. Babies can't tell time and someday you will have the time to spend everyday with him or at least take him with you." "Thank you mother, I don't know how to repay you for all you do for us with Patrick, what a God send you are." Mrs. Murphy thought to herself, you have it all wrong, you saved my sanity and gave me my life back with this little creature lying on his back, so peaceful in his crib. He is my main reason for living, except for my family, who put up with my blue period when I lost my mind.

CHAPTER 10

"SUMMER HEAT WAVE"

The summer of, 1942, was like a blast furnace, it seemed to everyone that spring hardly had a chance, when summer was heating up. Every tree and flower was in full bloom by Mother's Day, the farmers already had their crops in the ground. The green shoots made the corn and bean fields look like a soft green carpet over the earth.

Speedway City was all buzzing over the new store being constructed on Main Street, no one knew exactly what was going on. The Murphy's and the Ryan's were keeping a tight lid on the building plans, they planned a huge grand opening when it was completed. For the present there were canvas covers over the windows hiding the interiors of the two adjoining buildings. Even if you were in the green grocery store the doorways connecting the three buildings were covered over too. Mr. Mann was busy as was Mr. Piper the plumber, the excitement was contagious, and no one was to give out any information.

Red and John worked hard and long hours, it seemed to them that they hardly ever got to spend time with their little boy. Mrs.

Murphy always brought Patrick Joseph to the store everyday at noon for their picnic lunch. He loved to crawl around, but was confined to the blanket on the floor, there were just too many dangerous objects for him to get into. Red was sitting playing with her son, when Glenda Faye and Maggie came in, they too sat down and passed the little boy around. Red asked Maggie how she was feeling, Maggie said, "I am only half way to my due date and I already feel like I am ready to be done with this adventure, the heat is sweltering. At least at the hospital we have installed new cooling equipment on the maternity ward and that is heaven compared to being here." The other two girls laughed at their friend who sat there with her beautiful brown hair hanging in strings dripping with sweat.

Glenda Faye was at St. Elizabeth's with her mother who was visiting Sharon. They were sitting in the screened sun porch where you could catch a breeze if there was one. Sharon was in a good mood, she was laughing and playing cards with her mother, Mrs. Kelly loved her girls, they had a special bond. She saw Glenda Faye come in and motioned her over, "Sit down and play a few games with us," said Mrs. Kelly. Glenda looked at her younger sister, how radiant she was, smiling and happy. Glenda wondered how she handled this situation, having to give up her first child. There was no way, Glenda thought, that I could be so brave like this little slip of a girl was. The three women sat and sipped iced tea and had a wonderful visit together. These times were few and far between, everyone was so busy, Maggie and Red also came to see Sharon and bring her little boxes of candy and cookies, her favorite was oatmeal with raisins. Maggie and Sharon would stand side by side comparing their bodies to see who was growing the largest baby. So far, even with Sharon not being due until Thanksgiving, she was as large as Maggie who was due the last week of September or even the first week of October.

Josh and Ace were so busy with their air freight business, the General Motor's plant kept them on a full schedule. They had purchased two new airplanes and hired a few old army buddies to pilot them. Josh and Ace were eating lunch together at the hanger, Ace said to Josh, "Do you feel bad about not being physically fit for duty, I think about it all the time?" Josh replied, "Of course I do, especially since my accident was due to my own stupid nonsense. Sliding down the ship rails like a hero and busting my legs up, instead of doing it the proper way. Now, here I am with a lame leg that has left me with a limp forever." Ace, thought this over, his wounds were do to gun shots to the hand and shoulder while in the Pacific Islands, but he did not feel like a hero. "Well, said Josh, this company will not run itself, we had better get back to work." They both left the cool spot in the hanger, there were huge fans blowing there for the workers, and returned to the office. These two men and John were the best of friends, it was a time when you made friends for life and were always there to get their back, if need be.

Sadie Mann, Mary Kelly and Irene Murphy were sitting on the front porch of Sadie's home on Ford Street, they were planning a big 4th of July, party. There would be big chunks of ice brought in from the ice company on West Washington St., for the lemonade, iced tea and of course, the beer for the men. Mr. Bates had arranged for a large tent to be delivered, his brother owned a tent and awning business. Sadie thought back over the years to how many tents had been set up in her side yard. The girls graduation from high school, nurses training and many other holidays. Mrs. Kelly had Patrick Joseph on her lap, he was chewing on a cookie. Sadie watched the little boy and wished that her own grandchild would hurry and be brought into this world safe and sound. Irene was fanning herself with a large paper fan that had the name of the local funeral home printed on it. Mary Kelly said, "That fan gives me the willies, I wish you would put it away. I wonder why the drugstore or some other businesses do not give out fans?" These same fans were on every church pew at St. Christopher's Church.

Along with the plans for the 4th of July, the three women discussed plans for the yearly festival at their church. Sadie would cut all the onions, for some reason she never shed a tear when it came to this task. The onions would go into her famous coney sauce for the hundreds of hot dogs that would be sold. Irene always had charge of the baked beans, she and Minerva Bates were close friends and they also took care of the baked goods. When it came to baked macaroni and cheese, no one could come close to Mary's recipe, she had baked this dish for her eight children when that was all they could afford. Now it was a pleasure to do it for the church festival, there were never any leftovers to be taken home.

The main attraction at the festival was the fried fish sandwiches, the men were in charge of this operation. Sadie's husband Philip, worked in the open air breading tent, he first dipped the fish in a cream and egg wash, then into bread crumbs, back into the cream mixture and a second breading of crumbs. When his pans were full, Mr. Murphy would come by and take them to the cooking tent. Here there were three huge vats of bubbling oil, the whole operation went very quick, and the men had it down to an art. These same men normally never entered a kitchen, except to eat their meals at home. For some reason they seemed to love to don the tall white chef hats, made by the Great Aunts and the aprons to match. Each apron had St. Christopher's Church logo embroidered on the front panel.

CHAPTER 10

"DOG DAYS OF SUMMER"

The 4th of July party was a big hit, everyone on Ford Street came down to join in on the fun, but they loved Minerva's homemade cakes. She iced them with red, white and blue colors, some with flags and others with flowers and ribbon streamers. This little short and squat woman was like a machine, she never stopped, and nothing was too much to ask of her. The children ran around the yard and rode their decorated bicycles up and down the street.

The time was flying by, the festival came and went as well as the 4th of July, but the heat was oppressive. The farmers were worried that they might lose their crops to a draught if there was no rain soon. It was August, and Maggie was miserable with her pregnancy, Dr. Anthony wanted her to stop working and take it easy for the next month and a half. Maggie would not hear of it, she told him the hospital was her only escape from the heat. Dr. Anthony, laughed and said, "If that is the case we will set you up a bed and you can camp out here with your husband!" Maggie just looked at him and crossed her eyes, making him laugh even harder.

Red and John were working non stop on stocking the new stores, Mr. Murphy was home due to a summer cold. Red was standing on a step ladder when she called out to John, he turned and ran to grab her just as she fell. She had fainted due to the heat near the ceiling where she was working, John laid her down and went for help. Two of the ladies helping came running with cool water, they bathed the back of her neck and wrists with soft towels. Soon Red came around, she was stunned looking up at everyone staring at her. "You fainted," said John, Red was so embarrassed, she tried to get up , but she was still dizzy. "That is that, you are going home and rest for the next couple of days. You can spend some time with our son and get back on your feet," said John. Red knew he was right, she was no good to anyone in this condition. Finally the dizzy spell lifted and John drove his little stubborn red headed wife home for a good rest.

Glenda Faye was fixing supper and wiping the sweat from her face when Josh came home from the airport. He came over and spun her around and gave her a big kiss! "What was that for," Glenda asked? "For just being your wonderful, beautiful self. When I saw you standing there, your hair brushing your tiny waist, I just could not help myself," said Josh. He loved his wife to the point of being crazy sometimes, thank God for that hot day on the lonely beach in Dayton, Ohio. What were the chances of him being there and Glenda coming up out of the water, so like a mermaid?

Josh asked Glenda if she would like to eat outside on the back screened in porch, "Good idea," said Glenda. Josh got everything together and opened a bottle of red wine to go with the steaks Glenda was cooking. He sat the table and lit some candles, what a night, Josh thought. So many stars out, not a cloud in the sky, but he also remembered there were wells going dry and the crops were withering in the fields. Just for tonight, he sat that aside and waited for his bride to join him for a romantic supper.

Glenda looked at her husband, she too, loved Josh as much as he loved her. She lifted her glass of red wine and said, "Here is to a beautiful supper under the stars, thanks be to God for the new life that is to come into ours. The circumstances were dire for my sister, but wonderful for us, so here is to Sharon, may she find happiness in her future." This toast brought a mist to Josh's eyes, he thought about the tiny baby who was soon to be a reality and he too thanked God.

They were finishing up their meal, when there was a great clap of thunder, they both ran outside and looked up at the sky. There was a huge black thunder cloud with a magnificent bolt of lightning. Glenda Faye looked at Josh, and thought could this really be the rain they needed so desperately? Just at that moment, huge rain drops started falling, they just stood there until they were soaking wet. Glenda twirled around and around holding Josh's hands in hers. They started to laugh and dance like two woodland elves welcoming the life giving rain that summer night.

Red and John were at her mother's house, they were all finishing their supper, Mr. Murphy did not eat much, just some chicken soup, his cold was letting up finally. When they heard the huge clap of thunder, they grabbed up Patrick Joseph and walked outside just as the rain drops started to fall. The little boy thought this was great fun and squirmed to get down, he toddled around, falling every third step or so. Red and John let him play in the puddles that were forming on the concrete, John showed him how to splash with his tiny feet. Irene came to the door and watched the fun her family was having, she was glad for the cool air that was coming in with the rain.

Maggie was driving home from the hospital, the clap of thunder scared her, it had been so long since she had heard thunder, and she wasn't expecting it. Soon huge droplets of rain splashed on her windshield, the wipers made a muddy mess of the glass. It did not take long to clear, she rolled the window down and stuck her arm out to feel the cool rain on her skin. She could not wait to get home and celebrate the occasion with Ace. She hoped he would be home from the airport for a late supper. It was Thursday, so Maggie stopped at the green grocery to pick up some chicken to fry and potatoes to mash for supper. Now that the weather had broken she could let some cool air in and feel like cooking for a change. Sure enough, Ace's truck was in the driveway, Maggie took her time walking into the house, her bags were a soggy mess when she sat them down. Ace walked into the kitchen through the butler pantry, which still had no cabinets, due to the war contracts her father had to fulfill. Ace started to laugh when he saw his very pregnant bride dripping wet, he went to her and picked her up and spun her around. "Put me down, let me go," said Maggie. "You are soaking wet, go upstairs and change, I will put away the groceries and start peeling the potatoes," said Ace. He loved to help Maggie, they were a team, he was a modern man and kitchen work did not bother him in the least. He now knew how to cook more than just breakfast food.

The whole town of Speedway City was out on their porches, sitting and rocking while watching the wonderful rain that they had all been praying for come down in streams. The gutters were to overflowing, but no one seemed to care, the children were all running around splashing in the puddles and sliding down the wet grassy hills. Mr. and Mrs. Mann sat on their porch as well, her flowers were all but lost to the draught, and she hoped this rain would bring them back. She always had the prize winning roses at the county fair each year. That was not the case this year, her roses had a blight due to the hot weather and withered on their stems.

The next morning the sun came out bright, but the rain had brought in a cool front and everyone was happy to walk through the streets and enjoy the company of their friends. The grand opening of the new store was to be this evening at 6:00PM, so everyone would be home from work and enjoy the party. The Murphy's and Ryan's were ready, Maggie's father had done a wonderful job on the new sign already in place, but covered with a tarp. It was white with red and blue letters saying, "THE ONE STOP SHOP." They were so proud of their new business, they had games planned and many little prizes for the children. Red had ordered little sewing kits for the women and match books with their logo for the men, these were free for all who came into the store. There was also a coupon drawing for three months free groceries, to a limit of $5.00 per week. This was a big deal and there were many people who could use the prize, times were hard for some large families.

When 6:00PM, came Mr. and Mrs. Murphy along with Sandra Kay and John were waiting for the countdown to uncover the store fronts and the new sign. Five, four, three, two and one, everyone let out a sigh, the stores joined together as one with new swinging doors, it was beautiful, one lady remarked. When John made a little speech thanking everyone who came, he then opened the doors and handed out little shopping baskets to each customer to keep and bring back each time they shopped here. There were also new wire carts with wheels to push up and down the aisles, this was unheard of, but John had found them in a catalog, and thought them worth the money. The bigger the container, the more you can purchase, was his new motto. He used that on Red when he told her how much they had cost the corporation. Of course, the board had approved them, the male board members held a meeting when Red was off of work with her dizzy spells. It did not take long for her to forgive the men for not including her, they knew how frugal she was.

The opening was a huge hit with the whole town and surrounding areas. Maggie, Ace, Glenda Faye and Josh were all in attendance, for them to all be able to be in one place was a miracle. The three girls watched as the woman made over the two new stores, the unmentionable area was a big hit with the really young women. The older women liked the dry goods section and they sold three brand new sewing machines that very night. The Great Aunts were there with their new aprons on stating across the bib, "The One Stop Shop." They had made aprons for every employee, navy blue with red, white and blue letters. Each aisle had a number with little signs hanging from them saying what was in each aisle, this made shopping so much easier for their customers. Needless to say, this was state of the art shopping for 1942, it would go on to lead to bigger and better things for the Murphy's and the Ryan's.

CHAPTER 12

"SOME THINGS WILL NOT WAIT"

Due to the rain coming in and the cool weather that followed, the crops were saved and the harvest, though, a little short was still plentiful this year. September was here, the children had returned to school, where did the summer go most of them were thinking. So many children started school that year with new clothes and school bags and supplies from, "The One Stop Shop."

Maggie was working with Dr. Anthony the third week of September, they were operating, when Maggie noticed a constant cramping pain in her back. She put her hands on the small of her back and rubbed the worse spot, Dr. Anthony noticed her gesture. "Maggie, are you alright, you look so tired, when we finish, you are to go home and not come back until your labor starts, I am serious young lady," said Dr. Anthony!

Maggie was changing in the nurses lounge, she removed her clothes and stepped into the shower, the water felt good on her back. All at once she doubled over with pain, she knew at once she was in labor, but it was too soon! Maybe two or three weeks too soon, she dried off slipped on a clean hospital gown and her slippers. She went in search of Dr. Anthony, hoping he had not left the hospital yet. Maggie found Dr. Jacob Adams in the hall, he looked at her and put his arm around her waist to help her to the maternity ward where she could lay down. "I will have Lucas paged, using his first name, I believe he is still in the doctors lounge," said Dr. Adams. Maggie flagged down a nurse she worked with, she was surprised to see Maggie as a patient on her ward. "Come over to me, Opal, I need a pad and pencil for you to call my family." Opal went to get Maggie what she requested, Dr. Anthony came running through the door. He asked Maggie a few questions and one he could see had already happened. Her water had broken, she was wet from the waist down. Now the pains were coming faster, about 15 minutes apart, she knew her family would have time to get here, if they hurried.

Maggie was in hard labor when Ace and her mother walked through the door, the rest of her family and friends waited in the lounge as instructed. This was so hard for Red and Glenda Faye, they wanted so much to be right by Maggie's side and watch her baby's birth. They were both nurses, after all, that should pull some weight here in the hospital where they took their training. Red, being Red, went in search of the head nurse on duty, they turned out to be old friends. The nurse told Red, that she and Glenda Faye could wait outside of the labor room, that way Mrs. Mann or Ace could give them immediate updates. In 1942, not even the husband or mother could be in the delivery room, their only choice was to pace the floor after Maggie was wheeled to delivery.

Maggie was holding her mother's hand on one side and Ace's on the other. Her pains were coming fast now and Dr. Anthony was concerned with the early arrival of her baby being so premature. After examining Maggie again, he said it was time to go to the delivery room, the nurse gave Maggie a small whiff of gas to ease her pain. She said she did not want to be put out completely, she wanted to see her baby come into this world, just like her mother had.

Everyone outside said their good wishes to Maggie as she was wheeled by on her way to delivery. By this time she was racked with pain, she wondered how her mother had delivered a 9lb. baby at home without the aid of gas or ether. Maggie was told to push with each contraction, she had tears running down her cheeks, but they were happy tears, her baby was almost here. Finally, Dr. Anthony said, "One more big push, bare down, make it count, Maggie." Maggie did her best, she felt the baby slip out, and Dr. Anthony held her little tiny baby boy up for her to see. Maggie laid back against the pillow and prayed he would be safe and sound. The nurse took the tiny infant to a warm table and cleaned him up, he weighed in at just 5lbs. She wrapped him up and handed him to his mother. Maggie looked down at the little infant, she could not hold back the tears as she held his little hand in hers. "You and I, along with your daddy are going to have great adventures in the years to come, my little one," said Maggie. She could have sworn her baby smiled up at her with his big, Irish blue eyes.

Maggie was wheeled to her room and the nurse helped her brush her hair, she had the nurse open the bag her mother had brought to the hospital for her. "Please take out the blue ribbon in the side pocket and let me put it around my hair," said Maggie. The nurse opened the door to Maggie's room, in came Ace, Maggie's mother and her family and friends. Everyone was crying and carrying on about what a perfect little boy Maggie and Ace had brought into this world.

Maggie asked if everyone would mind leaving for a few minutes, she wanted some time with her mother, father and her husband. Sadie and Philip were there with Ace, Maggie looked up at the three of them and said, "I would like to name this little guy, Philip Harold VanCamp, if that is alright with everyone here?" Maggie's mother took the little boy in her arms and cried for the little boy she had lost many years ago, with the same name, Harold. Sadie looked at her husband, Philip, and said, "There will be no more blue January and February's for me. God has sent me an angel this day, with big blue Irish eyes." Ace did not know the story, but Maggie had plenty of time to fill him in later. Sadie handed little Philip to his father who was itching to get his big hands on him. Ace sat on the side of Maggie's bed holding the tiny boy, he slipped off his wedding ring and it slipped around Philip's little wrist. Maggie smiled up at her husband, how had he thought to do that. Ace said, "Now the three of us are married, we are an unbreakable ring of love forever."

Mr. and Mrs. Mann excused themselves to leave the new parents private time with their new son. Outside Sadie told everyone all of the details, she said there will be plenty of time for visits later. Maggie and little Philip Harold need their rest, they have worked very hard this day, being born is not an easy thing, but so rewarding when finished.

CHAPTER 13

"PHILIP HAROLD COMES HOME"

"No, not there, across the whole front porch, attach it with the wire I gave you," yelled Red to Glenda Faye! "Calm down, you are out of control, it is only Maggie and Philip Harold, not the queen of England and the crown prince," said Glenda Faye, with a smile on her face. Red was so excited, she could not wait for things to settle down, so she could get her hands on the baby, she love infants more that bigger children. Glenda Faye did all she could to contain herself, she knew that in just two months, she too would be holding a new life in her own arms. It sure was going to be a busy place here in Speedway City when it came to these three friends of the heart. Maggie was supposed to be on her way, her mother was upstairs preparing the nursery and fixing Maggie's room to welcome her home. She had four big bouquets of flowers delivered for the occasion, her husband thought she had gone a little overboard. As Sadie looked at all the little wooden toys, Philip Sr. and Austin Bates had made, she thought to herself, yes, he knows what overboard is!

Maggie had to spend one week in the hospital, they would have preferred her stay the full ten days, but she felt wonderful. She had no tearing or cutting during her delivery, which made all the difference in the healing process. Ace arrived right on time to fetch his bride and their new son, the nurse handed the baby off to Ace, while she helped Maggie into the wheel chair. They left the hospital with a whole cart of bouquets sent from friends at the hospital and in Speedway City.

Ace handed little Philip Harold to Maggie and walked around the automobile to the drivers side of the car. Ace got in and paused, he looked at his wife and said, "You have never looked so beautiful as you do this very moment, I will lock this in my memory forever. Your hair tied up with a blue satin ribbon matches the trim on the baby blanket." Maggie, blushed and smiled as she leaned over and kissed her husband and now the new father of her son.

When they pulled up in front of their home, the girls were climbing down off the ladders. The banner said, "Welcome home to the VanCamp family." Everyone came out to help Maggie into her home, she sat down in the big overstuffed rocker with her baby. Ace carried up her bags and found Mr. and Mrs. Mann putting the finishing touches on the nursery. Mr. Mann was hooking up a little lamp with cut out elephants on the shade. He explained that when the light was turned on the elephants would shine on the walls. Mrs. Mann had already left the room, she walked into the front room and lifted her grandson from her daughter's arms and sat down. As Sadie looked into those big blue Irish eyes, her own eyes misted over. She remembered her own little boy, Philip Harold, those many long years ago. He had been the best baby, never crying, just nursing and sleeping. She shook her head, she would not go back into the past, she knew that God had sent her little boy back to her in this new life that she was holding. It would be a secret that only she and God would share and she was thankful.

The company stayed for a short while and had refreshments with Maggie and Ace, they were both starving for a good home cooked meal. There was plenty of food, they all sat around the big wooden table that Maggie's father had made especially for her. Maggie had wanted a table that would grow with her family, just like her mother's. The ladies cleaned up and Sadie saw them all on their way. She would remain to help Maggie care for the baby the first week that she was home. Maggie was glad for the help, even though she knew babies from one end to the other. It was different when it was your own and you would be all alone sooner or later.

Sadie only woke Maggie up to nurse her baby and let her sleep the rest of the night. When Maggie was up, Sadie would lay down and nap for a few hours while Maggie bathed her little son. She marveled at every inch of this little miracle, he was so perfect, just very small. He had lost a few ounces while in the hospital, but would start to gain, now that he was home.

Ace came running through the door each night, he could not wait to hold his son and feed him some water or change his diaper. He was a modern father, he wanted to help in any way he could. He was better at taking care of the baby than cooking, so Maggie and Ace developed a routine that worked for them. They would wheel the basinet in the dining room during supper and usually Philip Harold would sleep during the meal. If not, one of the two of them would hold him on their lap and rock him. He was a very good baby, just like his namesake had been.

Maggie's baby shower had been postponed for two weeks due to Philip's early arrival. Today there was a house full of ladies and tons of gifts, many from the, "One Stop Shop," baby department. It was nice to know the gender of the baby, it made it easier to pick out little clothes and many colors of blue. Mrs. Murphy had knitted many little sweater outfits for the coming winter months. The Great Aunts had made a beautiful baptismal gown with a matching bonnet and blanket. There were many layers of soft handkerchief cotton and lace with ribbons that hung as long as the dress. The blanket had a wide satin banding, which would one day be little Philip's favorite blanket to drag around everywhere he went.

It seemed to Maggie that she would never get to the bottom of the pile of presents, but finally everyone was getting hungry and there was a huge cake, made by Minerva Bates. The cake was wonderful, it tasted of the best vanilla and had blue icing that melted in your mouth. She had made small baby booties out of the same blue icing and bows on each corner. All of the women brought a covered dish and Sadie had baked one of Mr. Bates' best hams for the special occasion. Usually this was saved for Christmas and Easter celebrations.

By the time everyone left and the girls had cleaned up the house and done the dishes, it was late in the evening. The men were coming in to collect their wives, they had been at a big poker tournament at Mr. Kelly's house. Finally when Maggie and Ace were all alone with little Philip, they had a chance to rest. They put the baby to bed and they too lay down for the night, Ace held Maggie in his arms and they all three fell into an exhausted sleep.

Maggie enjoyed her time at home with her child, she did not plan to return to the hospital for two months. Her mother would care for little Philip while she was at work, this was almost unheard of in 1942, but Maggie said she would lose her mind if she could not go to work. She was a different breed of liberated woman who enjoyed her work and felt gratified from the good she did to help others.

CHAPTER 15

"THANKSGIVING DINNER 1942"

The months seemed to pass by so quick, it was getting close to Sharon's due date and Glenda Faye was so excited. She had her own nursery ready, she had done it in soft green, pastel yellow and light brown. This way it did not matter if it were a boy or girl, she did not even care if it were twins, she just wanted her baby.

Thanksgiving was held at the Kelly's this year, Christmas would be at Mr. and Mrs. Mann's home as usual. Also, all three couples would celebrate their first anniversaries together with their children included this year. The weather was mild and everyone was seated at the big dining room table. The younger Kelly children were now old enough to be included, instead of having to sit at a children's table. Later, Mrs. Kelly was going to take Sharon a big plate of Thanksgiving turkey and the trimmings, so she would not feel left out.

The dinner was winding down when the telephone rang. Glenda Faye answered the telephone, she immediately hung up and ran into the dining room. "Everyone, that was Sister Francis from St. Elizabeth's, Sharon is in labor and things are not going well," said Glenda Faye. The girls got up, they would drive in one autobile and their husbands would bring Mr. and Mrs. Kelly along right behind them. The Murphy's and the Mann's would stay and take care of the children. The last thing they all heard was, "Call us as soon as you know anything."

Maggie was driving, Glenda Faye was a bundle of nerves and Red was praying allowed. She had not forgotten that she had been a nun just a short while ago. They pulled up and parked in Glenda Faye's reserved spot, being chairman of the board. They could see the new OBGYN wing almost finished as they entered St. Elizabeth's home for the unwed. The three girls were running to the antiquated delivery suite. Glenda Faye's shoes sounded like a hammer hitting concrete, she was running so fast. Maggie could smell blood before she could see it! Red was right behind them as they entered the room where sister Francis was holding Sharon's hand and telling her to push. Maggie could see the whole scenario was one big mess. The young doctor turned to Maggie with a look of fright on his face. He said, "I have done everything I know how to do, there is a problem, the baby will not come down." Maggie grabbed a gown and gloves, she pushed the doctor out of the way and sat down on the stool. She examined Sharon, who was screaming now, she was in the middle of a contraction. The rest of the family had arrived, the men waited in the hall with Mr. Kelly. Mrs. Kelly came to her young daughter's bedside and grabbed her hand and cradled her in her arms. Glenda Faye was on the other side of the Sharon holding her hand as Sharon squeezed it till Glenda thought it would be broken.

Maggie looked up at everyone in the room and said, "The baby's shoulders are caught on Sharon's pelvic bone, and the baby is too big. It is too late for a C-section that they we are not even set up to do here." Glenda said, "Do whatever you think is necessary to save their lives, you have our permission." Maggie looked at Red and told her to gown and glove, Red did as she was told. Maggie said, "I will have to numb her up and cut her to get the baby out before I lose the both of them. Red hand me a syringe full of Novocain and a scalpel."

Red took the little bottle out of the cabinet and filled the syringe full and handed it to Maggie, she numbed Sharon and then they had to wait a few minutes. With the next scream out of Sharon, Maggie asked for the scalpel and cut Sharon. The blood was flowing non stop, Maggie yelled, "Call St. Ann's, get an ambulance and a doctor over here and tell them to bring a large supply of blood." Maggie reached into Sharon and first freed one shoulder and then the other and the baby slipped out. Maggie saw that the umbilical cord was around the baby's neck, without saying a word she lifted it off and the baby immediately pinked up. Maggie breathed a sigh of relief and then she cut the cord. Red was there to receive the baby and wrap it up tight, there was not time for weighing and cleaning, and she wanted Sharon, Glenda Faye and Mrs. Kelly to see the baby.

Red was silently praying the Hail Mary the whole time, she laid the little baby in Sharon's arms, while Mrs. Kelly and Glenda Faye held Sharon in theirs. Maggie was packing Sharon with white towels and then started stitching her up. Red stood in the corner, she knew there were angels in the room, and she had a special connection with her God. She prayed, "Please, God, don't take this young girl, she has not yet begun to live." Red prayed this over and over.

Maggie looked up at Glenda Faye and said, "You and Sharon have a new baby girl." Everyone was crying, Sharon tried to lift her arms to give the baby to Glenda, but Glenda would not let her do this yet. "You hold her, let her see you, she has been silent, such a good baby already, just looking around at this new world." Sharon said in a soft whisper, "Would it be alright if we named her, "Shawnee Mary," after her father and our mother?" Glenda started to cry again, "Of course, whatever you like, she is ours and always will be ours, she is of our blood." Mrs. Kelly held her daughter and stroked the small infant's cheek, "She looks just like you when you were born, Sharon." Sharon asked that Glenda take the baby, that she was so tired, and Glenda did as asked.

Maggie was still working on trying to stop the blood, she had delivered the afterbirth, but the uterus was still pumping out blood in big gushing spurts. Red came over to Maggie and whispered, "For our ears only, there are angels here, Maggie, I am fearful for what is about to happen." Maggie looked up as she was pressing blood soaked towels against Sharon. She could hear the siren of an ambulance from a far off distance. "Thank God," she thought to herself.

Maggie asked Red to relieve her, she pulled off the gloves and gown and slipped into a clean gown and went to speak to Sharon and see the new baby that Glenda Faye was holding. Sharon asked for a priest, sister took off in a sprint and returned immediately, Father Hadley, he came in prepared and gave the young girl the last rites. Sharon closed her eyes as he anointed her forehead, eyes and lips. Father Hadley said all the prayers and then blessed both Sharon and the new baby.

Mrs. Kelly leaned down close to Sharon's mouth to hear what she was whispering, "Mother tell everyone I have to go home now, God has sent His angels, can't you see them, they are so beautiful," said Sharon. She took her last breath at the same time that little Shawnee Mary let out her first cry. Her mother's life force had transferred from her body to Shawnee Mary's.

The girls got the room cleaned up and then called the men in to say their goodbyes to Sharon and see the new baby. There would always be a forever sadness connected with Shawnee Mary's arrival.

CHAPTER 16

"SADNESS PREVAILS"

Everyone was gathered in the old antiquated delivery room, the young husbands had helped Mr. Kelly enter the room, he could barely walk on his own. Mr. Kelly went to his young daughter, Sharon, laying there looking so peaceful, like the angel she was to him. He only wished now, that she had been allowed to spend those nine months at home with the family. He never said aloud to anyone, but Sharon had a special place in his heart above the other Kelly children. Maybe because she was so like her mother, kind, gentle and loving to everyone she met.

Mr. Kelly could not help himself, he put his arms under his child and held her limp body next to him and cried deep racking sobs. Mrs. Kelly had never seen her husband like this, she motioned to Maggie to come to her. Just as Maggie got to Mother Kelly, the woman fainted in her arms. Red and John came and helped to take her out of the room and lay her down on a couch in the hall. Sister Francis brought cold towels and took over, she motioned the boys back into the room.

Maggie could now hear the running footsteps in the hall, the team from St. Ann's had arrived, but stopped immediately when they saw the scenario playing out in front of them. Maggie went to Doctor Jacob Adams, "We did all that was possible under the circumstances, if only the new wing had been completed, we could have saved her life!" said Maggie. Dr. Adams, was boiling angry, he said, "In this day and age there is no call for this barbarism to have occurred. This place will be shut down until the new hospital wing is completed and staffed properly." Maggie said, "Doctor, you cannot blame St. Elisabeth's for this, they have had little funding in the past. Not to mention the way society views unplanned pregnancy for young girls. They have nowhere to go and no one to care for them." Dr. Adams hung his head, he was just so angry and did not know what to do with this feeling.

The medical team was examining little Shawnee Mary, to make sure she was stable and in good health. They insisted that she be brought to St. Ann's for evaluation, but Glenda Faye would not hear of it. Glenda said, "I am a registered nurse, I can care for this child as well as you can, she is coming home with her mother and father and her grandparents this very day. Now if you will leave and excuse us we have many plans that need to be made."

Maggie and Red were so proud of Glenda Faye, it was very unlike her to lose her temper, but today was not a normal day. It was the worst and best day of her life. Ace went to Maggie, she looked like she had been wrung out and hung up to dry. He put his arms around his small wife and let her sob into his chest, he knew she was blaming herself partly for not being able to save Sharon. This was not true, Sharon was already dying when Maggie arrived, she knew that in her heart, but her mind would not let her believe it.

Red and John went into the hall and called the Kelly house, Red spoke with Sadie Mann, Maggie's mother. "Oh my, I don't know how to begin, Mrs. Mann, it was not good. We lost Sharon, Maggie tried to save her and the baby, but she could not save Sharon. The baby is good, Glenda Faye is bringing her home tonight. There will be no celebrating, but if you could just stay until we get home?" Mrs. Mann said, "Now, you listen here, Sharon Kay, you know me better than having to ask such a question. I will be here for as long as my best friend needs me. Mary Kelly and I are as one person, what she suffers I suffer and this will not be an easy task to overcome. Believe me I know what she is going through, I will try my best to help her overcome her grief, but she has to grieve if it takes a year. Now go back and assure Mary that I am here and will be here for her." "Thank you, Mrs. Mann and I am sorry if I upset you in any way." Said Red. "That is alright, I was a little harsh with you, but the truth of it all has not yet sank in for me, now, now my little girl, calm yourself and remember I love you." Said Mrs. Mann.

The staff from St. Ann's had left after they filled out all of their paperwork and made some arrangements for the Kelly's and what was going to be done with Sharon's body. Mrs. Kelly walked back into the room, she went to Sharon and kissed her forehead, you have gone home now my little girl, and you are no longer in this cold body. She then pulled the sheet over Sharon's face and turned and walked out of the room, followed by Mr. Kelly and the remaining people in the room.

Everyone went back to the Kelly home on 16th Street, Mrs. Mann had left it for Mrs. Kelly to relate what had happened with Sharon to her other children. There would have to be telegrams sent to the others that lived out of town and who were in the Armed Forces.

No one could help themselves, when Glenda Faye walked in with the baby, she was swamped by Kelly's, wanting to see their new niece. Glenda handed the baby to Mother Kelly and sat her in her old rocking chair, where she had rocked all of her babies over the years past. Glenda thought this would be the best medicine in the world for her right now. Mrs. Mann and Mrs. Murphy came over to make over the baby too. Mrs. Murphy said, "She looks so like her mother, a silent tear slid down her cheek." Mrs. Mann started giving orders, she asked Josh to go home and fill out the list she handed to him. She made it known that Mrs. Kelly would need Glenda Faye's help in the weeks to come and they would just have to stay here and help her get through this. Josh donned his hat and grabbed Ace and off they went to the Wakefield house. The two men were silent, then Josh said, "I have a daughter, I really have a little girl, thank you God." Ace patted his friend on the shoulder and was glad for him, he knew how much he loved his new son, little Philip Harold.

It was really late everyone had gone home, Mrs. Kelly had insisted that everyone who wasn't family had to leave. There were some hurt feelings, but they really understood grief, in the years past, everyone had been touched by death one way or the other. Glenda sat with her mother, she was still holding the baby, and Glenda reached for Shawnee, Mary held fast to her and finally loosened her grasp. " Mother, said Glenda, I am going to put the baby to bed, she has had a long hard time today being born and is sleeping like an angel."

Mrs. Kelly laid her face in her hands, she cried and sobbed till she thought her heart would break. She got up and went to the telephone and called Sadie, "I need you, my friend, I cannot do this without you here to hold my hand." Said Mrs. Kelly. "I will be right there," said Sadie. Sadie woke Philip, her husband and told him to get dressed, her friend needed her and she would be there for a few days. Mr. Mann dropped off his wife and walked her to the door with Sadie leading the way. She had her big woven basket full of all kinds of treats and little things. He had her valise and medicine bag in another hand. She kissed him at the door and went in without knocking. Mary Kelly ran and hugged her friend, Glenda stood at the top of the stairs and tears streamed down her face. She knew that was just the way she and her two friends, Red and Maggie were.

CHAPTER 17

"LIFE GOES ON"

The dawn broke with a beautiful sunrise, Sadie was in Mary's bedroom helping her dress for her daughter's funeral service. Mr. and Mrs. Kelly had decided that it would be a family viewing only and a closed casket for the rest who attended. She could not bare anyone looking at her young daughter and thinking anything wrongful about her. Everyone in town had guessed the cause of Sharon's sudden death and Glenda Faye having a brand new baby in her arms. "Mary, said Sadie, do you remember the day you dressed me when my little Philip Harold was taken home to be with God?" Mary said, "Of course, how could I not remember your sorrow, you couldn't even lift your arms, you reminded me of a figure in a wax museum." "That is the way I feel today, like I am melting from the inside out and soon there will be nothing but a puddle of feelings left on the floor." Said Mary. "Let us try to remember all the good things we can about Sharon, the games we played with her at St. Elizabeth's, how happy she was to have the baby for Glenda Faye. Her childhood, she was a blessing, one in a million children and a fine upstanding human being as a young lady. She, like so many right now are making the same mistake, seeing their loved ones off to this terrible war. I know in her mind, with that little diamond ring around her neck, that she thought of herself as married." Said Sadie. "My dear friend, you always have just the right thing to say to make me feel better. I will just have to pretend for a short while that she is just gone away, I cannot yet bare that she will not return to me. Skipping into my kitchen, putting the kettle on to boil for tea." Said Mary.

Everyone gathered at St. Christopher's church for the funeral mass and then there was a caravan of over one hundred automobiles winding around the streets of Indianapolis to arrive at Holy Cross Cemetery. There was a tent erected by Austin Bates to protect the family and close friends from the brisk November wind. Glenda Faye and her husband stood holding their little girl, she was wrapped in a pink knitted blanket that Mrs. Murphy had made for her. Maggie, Ace, Red and John were standing behind Glenda Faye's family, which was quite large now, with new wives being brought home for the first time, on such a sad occasion.

The priest said all the prayers and a friend of Mrs. Kelly's sang and old Irish song to send a soul on to heaven. Everyone close, laid a white rose of purity on Sharon's casket, as far as they were concerned, she was an angel now. Mrs. Kelly had her all dressed in white, just like a child making her first communion or a bride on her wedding day. Even in death, Sharon had a hint of a smile on her lips, she held her rosary and prayer book in her hands.

Glenda Faye was in a daze, her mixed emotions were driving her crazy and she knew she had to get hold of herself. She still had much to do, she had her husband and daughter who needed her. Thank God for Sadie, she was taking such good care of her mother and she knew just what to do to keep her in an uplifted spirit. The service was coming to an end with just a few townsfolk walking away. Glenda Faye caught sight of a woman sitting alone staring at Sharon's casket and tears were rolling down her cheeks.

Glenda Faye walked over with the baby still in her arms, she asked if she could help? The woman looked up and said, "My name is Marge McGill." That was all Glenda Faye needed to know, she quietly laid her daughter in Mrs. McGill's arms. "This is your granddaughter, her name is Shawnee Mary Wakefield. She is named after her father and her grandmother, I think you need to get to know her in the days and years to come." Said Glenda Faye.

The woman hugged the baby to her breast, and cried tears of joy and sadness for the loss of Shawnee's mother and father. The joy was for herself being included in the life of this new human being in her arms. "Thank you, I cannot express my gratitude for your kindness, you are a saint." Said Mrs. McGill. "That I am not, said Glenda Faye, but kind I am, my own mother taught me that from the time I was born." Mrs. McGill handed little Shawnee Mary back to Glenda Faye and said, "You contact me, and I don't want to interfere in any way. My husband is out of town, he will be so thrilled when I tell him about what happened here today." Said Mrs. McGill. Glenda Faye invited Mrs. McGill back to the Kelly house for the wake, she wanted her to meet her mother, Mary. Mrs. McGill said she could not, she did not know anyone who would be there. Glenda Faye said in a stern voice, "Being a part of this family is getting to know one another and all of our friends. You must come, my mother will welcome you with open arms, I will bet you and her other two friends will include you in their circle of friendship." That was that, Mrs. McGill was officially adopted into the little circle of friendship in Speedway City, Indiana.

The wake was held at the Kelly home on 16th Street, there were people coming and going all afternoon. There was so much food and of course a beautiful cake baked by Minerva Bates that said in pink icing, welcome to our new angel. This was a play on words, you could take it to mean the angel was Sharon or Shawnee Mary. Knowing Minerva, she liked to keep people guessing, even at a wake. The Irish are a jolly group, there was music and even dancing, the men were taking many trips to the back porch for a breath of air, but that was where the big tubs of iced beer and bottles of Irish whiskey were located.

There was no time to be sad at an Irish wake, celebration was on the menu and that was what you did. Even Mr. Kelly came over and asked his wife for a turn around the floor to the song, "When Irish Eyes Are Smiling." Sadie looked at her best friend smiling up at her long time husband, still in love after all these years, it warmed her heart. She turned to Philip and asked if he thought the young couples would know the kind of love that they shared? Philip hugged Sadie and said, "Of course, we raised our girls to be good women with high morals, integrity and most important love in their hearts. They, the three of them standing there together, do you know what they are mother? Said Philip. "No, answered Sadie." "They are true friends of the heart, and they don't come any better than that! Said Philip.

CHAPTER 18

"NO TIME FOR TEARS"

Things began to settle down after the funeral and wake were over. Sadie stayed on at Mary's house for two weeks, they were such good friends that each one knew the other's wish before it was said aloud. There was something bothering Sadie, the two youngest Kelly children, Beverly and Paul were having a really hard time with the death of their sister, Sharon. She talked to Mary about this, but she had no idea what to do for them to help ease their pain. Sadie said, "I have an idea, but let me run it by John and Sandra Kay first."

Mrs. Mann stopped in to see Red and John at the, "One Stop Shop," they were busy working in the store room. Sadie relayed the problem with the children to Red and John, she told them that she thought maybe an after school job of some kind would help clear their minds. "What a wonderful idea, we could use Beverly to cashier for us and Paul could help John and Mr. Murphy stock the shelves." Said Red. Sadie thanked the young couple and left to go home, she had been away for so long staying with Mary. Everyone had made sure that Mr. Mann was well taken care of,

Maggie and Red cooked for him and cleaned the house in her absence.

Sadie called Mary and told her of the plan, Mary was overwhelmed with gratitude and thought it would be perfect. Mary said, "I know you have always held a special place in your heart for Paul, as have I, he is my baby." "Yes, I love all of your children, but little Paul grabbed hold of me on the first day he was born and never let go," said Sadie. Sadie's husband came in from the lumberyard, he hung up his cap, came over and gave his wife a great big hug. He was so glad that she was back in their home, he had been so lonely, and they had not spent very many nights apart since they were married. He understood fully that Mary needed his wife and he was glad for the kind of woman he had married. Sadie was like a rock, his rock and everyone who might need her.

Maggie, Red and Glenda Faye were having a rare lunch at the drugstore together, with the children there was no extra time for just girl meetings these days. The weather had turned extremely cold for early December, this meeting was to discuss the big Christmas and Anniversary party to be held at Mr. and Mrs. Mann's home. Maggie sat back and looked at her two friends, her heart ached for Glenda Faye and Red, they were so special to Maggie. "What are you thinking about, Maggie?" asked Red. "Oh, nothing special just how much I love the two of you and how our lives have changed so fast. Here we are three old married ladies all with babies of our own." Said Maggie. The three girls ordered their ice cream sundaes, they all three stopped immediately and looked at each other with puzzlement on their faces. Red said, "Oh my Lord, we all ordered different flavors for our sundaes, could it be possible that we are all pregnant?" Maggie sat there silent, she thought how could that be, I have a two month old baby, but her monthly dates were not regular. Glenda Faye said, "You know I cannot have children, why would you think that?" In her mind, Glenda thought, the doctor said most likely, he did not say, positively you cannot have children. "I think we all better make doctor appointments, it would be wonderful if we had our babies at the same time. I do feel sorry for the two of you having brand new babies and another so close together." Said Red.

Glenda Faye made an immediate appointment with Dr. Jacob Adams, she did not mention anything to Josh about being pregnant. Glenda was still sitting on the leather table with her gown on when Dr. Adams came back into the examining room. "Well, young lady, it looks like you are having a miracle baby according to Dr. Anthony. He told me you had a tilted uterus and probably would not conceive, but you have proved him wrong." Said Dr. Adams. Glenda was walking on air when she left the doctor's office, she knew she had seven or eight months to prepare for taking care of two babies. Now, to tell Josh first and then her friends. She was stopping to pick up two steaks and all the trimmings for a romantic supper for the two of them.

Red and Maggie both went to see Dr. Anthony on the same day, they both got the same news, "Young ladies you two will have your babies at the same time. I believe your friend will be joining you and making it a trio of mothers to be. Just don't go into labor at the same time, I would sure have my hands full." Said Dr. Anthony. Red and Maggie walked out of the office not saying a word, when all at once, they started to giggle and it turned into full blown laughter. "Wait until Glenda Faye hears the news, Josh was over the rainbow with her news, now we have ours. Oh my, we have two men to tell first, maybe we should take a clue from Glenda and make them a great dinner to break the news." Said Red. Maggie agreed, she wondered how Ace would take the news with having little Philip Harold who was only two months old. She knew her mother would be pleased, it was the old way, when God gave you a baby, and you were grateful and happy.

Maggie and Red went to the store, they were worried that John would be there and they did not want him to know what they were up to. The butcher told them John was out on a delivery and would be back in about an hour. They each bought steaks, with the price of meat these days, it took a week's grocery budget to pay for them, but the girls did not care. Maggie was the most worried, Red's little boy would be two years old when she had her baby, which was not hard to deal with. Maggie knew what her mother would say, "Maggie, you are having Irish twins, that is two babies not a year apart in age." Maggie was good at doing more than one thing at a time, she knew she would have to quit her job at the hospital, she just could not juggle that many jobs at once. She would miss working, but maybe she could volunteer part time at the new OBGYN wing at St. Elizabeth's when it was completed.

After what had happened to Sharon at St. Elizabeth's, Maggie was brought before the board at ST. Ann's Hospital. There was an inquiry, but with Maggie being a registered nurse and midwife, she was not found guilty of any wrong doing. The young resident doctor who had been called to attend to the birth of Sharon's infant, also backed up Maggie's testimony. He told the board that without Maggie, he would have lost both the mother and the infant. St. Elizabeth's was not shut down, but no more deliveries would be preformed there until the new hospital wing was completed and properly staffed. The building was almost ready to open, they were looking at the first of February, according to Glenda Faye, who was board of director.

Maggie dropped Philip Harold off at her mother's house for an over night stay, she wanted her evening with Ace to be private, without any interruptions. She was not quite sure how Ace would take the news of her pregnancy. Maggie remembered back to the night she took her husband in her arms and asked him to make love to her. He asked if it was too soon for this, she answered that she felt wonderful and did not want to wait the six weeks for her final check-up with the doctor. She was trying to figure out exactly when her due date would be, it was too early for the doctor to calculate. She did know that it was about three weeks after the birth of Philip that she and Ace had their first romantic night together and being a Catholic there was no birth control used.

Ace came home from the airport and went straight to his wife, he kissed her and then he saw the candles lit in the dining room. He smiled and said, "Looks like I might get lucky tonight, where is our son?" "Our son is at his grandmother Mann's house for the night, it is just you and I for dinner tonight." Said Maggie. Ace left the kitchen and went upstairs for a nice hot shower, the weather was turning very cold and he loved to feel the hot water running over his body. He also wanted to be clean and smelling good for his little wife, he wondered what was up, he knew Maggie very well and the candles meant something special.

After they were seated, Maggie poured Ace a cold glass of wine and she stayed with water for her meal. Ace commented about her not joining him with a glass of wine. "Well, said Maggie, if I am right on my dates, next 4th of July we will probably be having another firecracker of a child to play with Philip." Ace put down his glass, stood up and came around the table to his wife. Maggie was looking sheepishly at Ace, she did not know what to expect from him. "Maggie, I love you and Philip more than my own life, now you are giving me one more reason to love you even more. Please, just make this one a little girl, I so want a daughter to pamper and be a daddy's girl, just like you are." Said Ace. Maggie put her arms around Ace and started to cry, these were tears of joy, she had shed too many tears of sadness lately. The couple ate their dinner and then went up the stairs hand in hand, they would lay together and discuss their future with two children.

When John came home from the store he was greeted by a room full of streamers and balloons, his wife had on one of those funny paper hats. John started to laugh, the sight of his tiny wife standing there as if she were attending a birthday party was so funny that he could not help himself. "John, stop laughing at me, this is a serious occasion." Said Red. "Well, maybe you better clue me in so I can stop laughing and where is my son?" "Your son is next door, he is spending the night with his grandparents, he is not part of this party tonight." Said Red. John took off his heavy coat and hat, he walked to the dining room and there were even more decorations. He could smell steaks cooking, he was totally puzzled by all that was taking place in his home.

Red came in with the rest of the meal and sat down across from John, she, like her friends poured wine for her husband. "I cannot stand it one more moment, what in the world is going on with you tonight, Red?" said John. Red got up and came over and sat on John's lap, she whispered in his ear, "Happy 4th of July." John looked at Red, now he thought she had lost her mind completely. Red stood up and turned sideways, she asked John, "Will you still love me when my stomach sticks way out here, as she moved her arms further out from her body?" John stood up so quick that he turned his chair over backwards, he took his wife in his arms and kissed her all over her face and neck. "You mean it, you are pregnant?" said John. "Yes, the date is not exact, but pretty close, now Patrick will have a brother or sister this coming summer." Said Red. John was beside himself with joy, he looked at his wife, he had a worry cross his face that he hid from Red. He thought about how tiny she was and what had just happened to Sharon. He voiced his concerns with his wife. "John, look at all the small women in our church, marching in with five or six children, don't worry about this until there is something to worry about!" said Red. "I am sorry, I just love you so, if anything were to happened to you because of my actions, I could never forgive myself." Said John. "Stop right there, no more sad talk, this is a celebration, we are going to have a beautiful child together. Well, maybe not just the two of us, Maggie and Glenda Faye are also pregnant." Said Red. This was a little too much news for John, he just sat there shaking his head. "Don't you three ever do anything alone, I might have known it would be a group effort?" said John.

CHAPTER 19

"THE WAR CREEPS INTO SPEEDWAY CITY"

The girls were gathered at Mrs. Kelly's for a luncheon with their mother's, this was a pleasant surprise for Sadie, Mary and Irene. With the busy schedules of everyone, it was hard to get everyone in one place for very long. When Sadie and Mary saw a cake baked by Minerva Bates in the middle of the table, they knew something was up. The three girls felt as if they were those three little girls again, not grown women. They had chosen Red to speak for them, she knew no fear and had a great way with words. Everyone was seated, Red stood up and said, "We are all three pregnant." Then she sat down, so much for a way with words, and breaking the news in a gentle way.

Mary, Sadie and Irene were speechless, they just sat there and said nothing. Glenda Faye asked, "Anyone for punch?" This broke the ice, there was so much kissing and hugging going on in the room. Each woman felt as if the girls belonged to them, they could not be separated in any way. This is the way it had always been since they were born. Mary said, "It is so like when Sadie, Irene and I were pregnant with the three of you, just weeks

81

apart." The joy and happiness overflowed that day in December, they decided not to tell anyone else until the Christmas Eve celebration. Sadie said, "Maybe I need Minerva to make three cakes for Christmas, Anniversary and one with baby booties on the top." Everyone laughed and they enjoyed their luncheon and drank their share of punch.

Mary Kelly sat in her rocker after everyone left, she thought of the new baby, Shawnee Mary, the light of her life. Now there was to be another child coming in the Summer, once again her house would be filled with small children. She had grown lonely roaming around her large home, that Glenda Faye had built for her. She knew her husband would be so happy when he heard the news, just two more weeks, she could keep the secret until Christmas Eve.

Sadie and Maggie rode home in Maggie's automobile, they went into Sadie's house together. "Mother, I know exactly what you are going to say to me, it is the old saying about Irish twins." Said Maggie. "Not so, I was going to tell you how proud I am of you, and also your friends. You have become upstanding women, true friends of the heart!" said Sadie. Maggie began to cry, her mother wrapped her arms around her daughter and they cried together. "Don't worry, my little Maggie, I will help you through this, it is quite a load for you and Ace to carry right now. You know your daddy will be so happy, but a little worried about your health, having two babies so close," said Sadie. Maggie looked at her mother with so much love in her heart, she kissed her good-bye and through an, "I love you," over her shoulder as she ran down the steps.

Red and her mother were having tea in the parlor watching Patrick Joseph, or, "Joey," as his grandfather now called him, as he walks around all the furniture. Irene looked at her redheaded daughter with the huge sparkling green eyes, she loved her so much it hurt her heart. Red's hair was grown out now since her return from the Pacific Island, Red liked it shorter than most women were wearing their hair. She told her mother many times that it was freeing and she bet someday all women would wear their hair in a shorter style. "Mother, you had better get those knitting needles out again, you will have quite a few sweaters to make for next fall when our babies will be just a few months old," said Red. Irene just smiled to herself, she was so glad that God had lifted her insanity so that she could enjoy the best of her life to come.

Ace was at the, "One Stop Shop," visiting with John and Josh. The three men all wanted to tell the other about the pregnancy, but their wives had sworn them to secrecy. John, said, "I cannot keep this to myself one more minute, Red and I are going to have another baby, now Patrick will not be an only child." Josh and Ace started to laugh, John did not see the humor, and until they both blurted out, "So are we!" The three men all looked astonished, but knowing their wives and how they never did anything alone, it did not surprise them in the least. "Now, you know we have to keep this a secret until Christmas Eve," said Ace. They knew the celebration would be big this year, with the grandparents and the great aunts in attendance.

John was telling Josh and Ace about the latest rationing of coffee and a few other items. Josh and Ace told John they too had rationing on items they delivered at the airport, but they could not go into detail because of government contracts. One of the men said, "What is next, shoes?" He did not know, but that was coming to. There were many women in Speedway City that already formed guilds to promote the war effort.

Sadie, Mary and Irene transformed the basement of the union hall into a sort of thrift store. You could bring your outgrown clothing, shoes, toys, etc., to be shared by those in need. When the rationing started it took off like a fire storm through the whole of America. The ladies wanted to make sure that no one did without when it came to the basic needs of their children and the family as a whole. Mr. Mann and Austin Bates built shelves and racks for the women in their spare time from old used wooden pallets donated from Josh and Ace. There was so much packing material that could be reused and Mr. Mann and Austin knew just how to transform these items into useful products.

John and Mr. Murphy donated to Sadie's women's league with grocery items that were just a little too old to sell in the store, but still good enough to make a meal from. It was items like sugar, coffee and spices that were hard to obtain, because of importing these goods. Of course, Sadie had an answer to this problem, everyone who lived without children, husbands or wives, would donate part of their rations to the food bank. The women would repackage these items and give them to the needy. Sadie and the women would laugh when they pulled out a tea bag that was dried and then they would reused it one more time. It was a time when women Sadie's age remembered the great depression and they were still thrifty.

You could not walk around Speedway City or downtown Indianapolis without seeing so many young men in uniform. The young girls went crazy over the men in the sailor suits, the men looked so cute to them. There was really nothing cute going on, it was war and soon these young sailors would be shipping out to the Pacific to fight the Japanese. There was a boom in the sale of American flags, there were all sizes. It seemed to most people that they could not remember a time when all of America had come together as one. It was a shame that it was because of a World War, there were many that still lived who fought in the First World War.

Sadie, Irene and Mary were so busy, with babysitting and their women's league, but the Christmas Party needed to be planned. The great aunts were so excited, they made many of the table decorations and would be bringing their special side dishes that everyone would be expecting. Sadie wasn't so sure of the house expanding to hold everyone this year, but God would take care of that for her. The VanCamps would be coming and the Wakefield's were coming too. That is only four more, Sadie thought, she could handle it and who ever else wanted to stop by. Mary stood up, so unlike her, she was a timid soul and never went against the grain of anything. "I think we should move this party to my huge house, just for this year. I have so much room that is going to waste," said Mary. The three women finally came to the agreement that this was a good idea, Irene said she would make all the telephone calls and let everyone know about the change. Sadie did not say anything, but it was really a great relief for her.

The, "One Stop Shop," was doing a booming business the week before Christmas. They had even brought in new shinning bicycles for the girls and boys and crying baby dolls for the little girls. Every time Red walked by a small girl holding one of the dolls, she thought of her own baby growing in her womb and smiled. Red was glad that they had hired the Kelly children to help in the store, they were on break from school and working as hard as the adults. Opening this triple shopping outlet in Speedway City, was one of the greatest ideas ever, thought Red, as she walked around greeting all the shoppers. Mrs. Murphy was in the back storeroom gift wrapping presents for men who were all thumbs when it came to doing this for their wives. This was her own idea and she loved being of help to John and her daughter, she kept Patrick Joseph in his playpen right beside her. He was a good little boy, he kept busy stacking his wooden blocks and playing with his other toys. When he got tired, Mrs. Murphy would change him, give him a bottle and he would go right off to sleep.

There was a big sign in the window of the shop that read, "Closed from Christmas Eve to the day after Christmas." Everyone knew they had to stock up on all of their Christmas groceries and shopping the day before Christmas Eve. The only stores open on Christmas Eve, were downtown Indianapolis. When the Murphy's closed up the store for the evening, they decided to walk home and let John and Red take Patrick with them. The evening was mild, they were staying open until 8:00Pm, every night until Christmas Eve. There was a smell of snow in the air as the older couple walked slowly up Main Street to there turn off on 15th Street. "Remember, Joseph, when we were a young couple walking downtown Christmas shopping. The weather was mile just like this, we were so in love and I was pregnant with Sandra Kay. Life was beautiful, just like it is now, God just keeps giving and giving?" said Irene. Mr. Murphy, put his arm around his wife, he was glad her bad times were behind her, he had missed her when she went away in her own mind for those few years.

CHAPTER 20

"CHRISTMAS 1942"

Finally, the big afternoon celebration was starting at the Kelly house. The Ace and Josh had left to go pick up the great aunts and one of their friends on leave from the Navy. The young man had no family to celebrate with and Josh would not hear of a service man being alone on Christmas Eve. The women were all gathered in the kitchen making sure everything was being well prepared. There was a turkey and one of Mr. Bates' wonderful hams sitting on the sideboard. Mrs. Kelly's big iron stove was full to the brim with side dishes to go along with the ham and turkey. Sadie and Irene were preparing their salads and desserts, the whole house smelled of Christmas.

The grandfather's kept an eye on the children and the young women tended to the babies. John was playing on the floor with a toy train that Patrick had ripped open before he could be caught. There was Mr. Mann's famous eggnog standing on a large round table in the entrance way of the house. Anyone who stopped by would be greeted and given a cup to celebrate the holiday and invited to stay if they wanted to. The men in these three families were good to help, they did not just sit back and let the women do all the work of entertaining. Maybe that was why their marriages were firm and long lasting.

Maggie went to answer the door, there was Josh and Ace, loaded down with presents and food dishes. The Great Aunts were following behind assisted by a handsome you man in Navy whites. Wow, thought Maggie, now there is a catch and she went looking for Beverly Kelly to entertain him. Forever the match maker, Maggie thought of herself, but I had better remind Beverly of her sister's problem. No, I will do that later, this is Christmas Eve, nothing like that would happen anyway. Maggie went in search of the young girl and introduced the couple to each other. She could see stars in Beverly's eyes, those Navy boys, she knew Glenda Faye had her own Navy officer as a husband.

Mr. and Mrs. Wakefield arrived along with Mr. and Mrs. VanCamp. Sadie walked into the entrance hall and helped everyone off with their outer garments. She was so grateful that Mary had offered her home for this special occasion, there were so many people this year. As she walked into the living room she saw that the pile of presents under the tree was growing by leaps and bounds. Patrick was already playing with the wooden train that her husband and Austin Bates had made for him. She stopped and just gazed around the room, her thoughts went back to a snow covered Christmas Eve when the girls had a visit from a beautiful lady and man in a big black automobile. Fate is a funny thing, now they were both here and they were Maggie's in-laws and the grandparents of little Philip Harold. Sadie shook her head and was back to the present and could hear everyone talking at once.

It was time to eat, the dining room had been turned into a cafeteria by Mr. Mann and Austin. The had built a three sided table for everyone to be able to sit together. After everyone found their place cards, written so beautifully by the Great Aunts, they were seated. Glenda Faye had been elected to make the announcements, she stood up and tapped her water glass with her spoon. Everyone stopped talking and paid attention to Glenda Faye.

"First, I want to thank everyone for attending our celebration this Christmas Eve. As you well know, it is also an anniversary party for myself, Maggie and Sandra Kay, and our husbands. Where has this year gone, we all three have children this year, which makes our parents so happy. I have a bit of a surprise for the whole crowd that I hope will top off our celebration. Maggie, Sandra Kay and I are all pregnant, we will be having our babies around the 4th of July," said Glenda Faye.

There was silence, Glenda Faye, was surprised at this, then everyone started standing up and clapping and wishing the happy couples good luck. Glenda Faye let out a sigh of relief, her father came to her and held her hands in his large hands and said, "My lovely young daughter, God knew what He was doing when He sent you to us. I love you, your mother and I wish only good things for you and your husband, now and in your future lives together." Glenda laid her head on her father's chest and let her tears fall on his shirt, this was a rare moment for her. Mr. Kelly did not say much, but when he did, you know it came straight from the heart.

The Great Aunts had on their paper Christmas hats and their little whistles, they were blowing them in and out making Patrick giggle. He was having a big time sitting in his high chair that Mr. Mann had made just for him. The Great Aunts had hand painted teddy bears and little lambs on the back and front of the chair. Patrick had potato salad and baked beans all over his face and bib. Red knew better than to try to keep Patrick clean until after the meal was over. The Great Aunts would keep feeding him until he started shaking his head, meaning he was finished with eating and wanted down.

Everyone gathered around sitting on the floor and furniture, where ever was comfortable for them. The presents were passed around and being opened and held up for everyone to see. By the time all the wrapping paper was picked up and the presents put into bags or left under the tree, it was time to go to mid-night mass at St. Christopher's Church.

The VanCamp's and Wakefield's stayed home to care for the children, who were already sleeping soundly. They would go to mass tomorrow morning, while everyone else slept in, if that was possible. When everyone walked out of the Kelly house there was a heavy snowfall on the ground. The snowflakes were large, just as they were last year. It was a prefect Christmas Eve celebration, God was smiling on the troop of people coming to welcome His son to earth this Christmas night.

CHAPTER 21

"A NEW IDEA FOR A NEW YEAR"

When midnight mass was over, everyone went their separate way. Philip and Sadie took the Great Aunts to their house, they would spend the next week with them, until after their New Year's Eve party. Glenda Faye and Josh picked up Shawnee Mary, against her grandmother's wishes to let her stay. They wanted her home for her first Christmas morning with them, there were presents under the tree from Santa to be opened by her parents. The Murphy's rode home with Red, John and Patrick Joseph, John let them out at the front door of their home and then drove next door to their house. Patrick Joseph was sleeping so sound that he did not wake up when Red laid him in his crib that early Christmas morning. Patrick, too had many presents from Santa under their tree. Maggie and Ace wrapped Philip Harold up like a little pea in a pod, the weather was really getting cold, but the snow had stopped for the time being.

When Philip walked his wife and the Great Aunts into the house, he then went back for three more trips to retrieve the presents and the food parcels sent home with them. The three women were boiling water for tea in the kitchen when he came in covered with large flakes of snow. He told them this was the last of the goods and was glad to get in out of the cold. They tried to get him to have a cup of tea with them, but he told them he just wanted to go to bed and get warmed up. Sadie poured a shot of Irish whiskey, some sugar and a drop of lemon juice in a large mug and filled it with hot water, she took this to her husband, who was sitting on the side of the bed. "I thought you could use a, hot toddy, to help warm you and let you have a nice peaceful sleep. You have worked so hard making this Christmas Eve celebration the best yet, I want you to know how much I love you," said Sadie. Philip looked up and smiled at his wife, he thought that he was the one who should be thanking her.

Christmas Day broke with bright sunshine and fresh fallen snow, all at once in the Kelly household, there were screams of delight. Paul was pulling his parents out of bed and waking the whole house. Beverly came out in her new pink robe and slippers given to her by Red and John. Paul said, "Come down, see what Santa has left us, you won't believe it!" There by the large pine tree sat two new bicycles, one was black and chrome, the other pink and chrome. Even though Beverly was almost seventeen, she was so excited, her old bicycle had been handed down many times. Mr. Kelly had one of his friends in the auto body repair business, paint the bicycle pink for Beverly. Paul was sitting on his bike, as he called it, turning the light on and off and ringing the bell. Each bicycle had a large basket on the front, which would come in handy bringing home groceries and other packages from the store. The two Kelly children ran over and hugged their parents, they loved them so much, not for the presents, but because they were so good to them.

All over Speedway City this same scene was playing out, little children were tearing open presents from Santa Claus. Their mothers were fixing a big breakfast feast of leftover ham, eggs and pancakes. The smell of Christmas was still heavy in every house and in their hearts.

Sadie was up early, she was not one to sleep in, but Philip was still in bed. The Great Aunts were sitting at the table helping Sadie with breakfast, they were chopping potatoes to fry and slicing ham. Rose, the youngest aunt looked up and said, "I have an idea, finding out about all the girls being pregnant, got me to thinking. There are no pretty maternity clothes, most women make do with old smocks or dresses gathered at the neckline. Since we still have our shop downstairs, why don't we hire four or five women who need to work with their husbands overseas. We could make pretty maternity clothing, what do you think?"

Lena and Beana looked up at Rose, as if to say, have you lost your mind. Lena spoke first, "We are in our eighties, what are you thinking?" Rose looked her straight in the eye and said, "Yes, we are that old, but we are not dead yet, we still have so much to offer. Just a week ago you were complaining of being bored and that you missed the millinery shop. I don't care what the two of you do, I am doing this. What do you think Sadie?" Sadie was at the stove, she thought to herself, stay out of it, you know better than to come between these three women. "I think if Rose wants to work, she should work, that doesn't mean the two of you have to follow her lead," said Sadie.

Philip came in the kitchen and poured himself a cup of Sadie's famous coffee, he liked his coffee strong and black. Immediately with the silence, he knew he had better excuse himself and go to the front room and turn on the radio for the latest news.

Finally, Lena and Beana, could not let their little sister get the better of them, they agreed to go into business once again. "It will be an adventure," said Rose. Sadie called Philip to the breakfast table, they filled him in on all the plans for the new shop. He volunteered to help them in any way he could, he and Austin could build almost anything they would need. The Great Aunts were so happy and excited, Rose ate her breakfast and went to get some paper and pencils. She was the artist in the trio, she sketched three smocks with matching skirts, when the other women saw the skirt they burst out laughing. There in the front was a big hole with ties to cross over the stomach. "What are you laughing at, where do you think the ladies would put their ever growing stomachs, I like my invention. You could have a black, brown and navy blue skirt that would go with many different colored smocks." Said Rose. Sadie agreed with Rose, it was genius, why hadn't anyone thought of this before now. No more huge flowing dresses to get in the way when you are cleaning or chasing after little children.

Lena chimed in, "I saw some beautiful material just the other day, downtown in one of the large department stores." "No, we will buy wholesale from New York by catalog, that way we will make a bigger profit." said Beana. Sadie stood back, she loved these women and could not imagine them not being in her life. She walked over and gave each one a big hug and kiss on the cheek.

Philip knew the four women in the kitchen would be working on this all day, if he did not remind them that it was Christmas Day. There would be company coming in and out, their son and his wife would be over. They had spent Christmas Eve with her parents, they too had a family tradition. Philip's other son and his wife was in Georgia where he was stationed in the army. Philip prayed every night that God would keep his youngest son safe from harm and the war would soon be over. Little did he know what was about to break lose in Europe that would take in the United States of America.

CHAPTER 22

"WELCOME BABY NEW YEAR 1943"

The week between Christmas and New Year's Eve, was a busy time at Sadie's home. The Great Aunts were so excited about the new adventure they were pursuing, they had designed and cut patterns for five maternity outfits. When Maggie stopped by with little Philip Harold, the first questions she asked was, "Can you make me slacks, I love wearing pants and always have?" The aunts looked from one to the other, they shook their heads in disbelief, but they new their great niece too well to say, "No," to her. Rose was a modern woman for being in her eighties, she stepped up and started taking measurements immediately for Maggie's new slacks. Maggie had to laugh when she saw the designs with the big round hole in the front of the skirt and now the slacks. "What did you think we were supposed to do with your belly when it starts to grow?" said Aunt Lena. Sadie watched the three women talk to her daughter, there was so much love and friendship in her kitchen, it brought tears to her eyes. Sadie shifted little Philip from one hip to the other and went on stirring the kettle of chicken soup.

Everyone had decided that since Christmas Eve had been a grand affair, that they would all three have New Year's Eve with their immediate families. Red and John had Mr. and Mrs. Murphy to their house for the traditional boiled ham, cabbage, potatoes and carrot pot luck dish. It was thought to be good luck to have ham and cabbage for the New Year. The three young couples needed some time alone, so this year they would cook the meal on New Year's Eve and spend the actual holiday by themselves with their children. Maggie, Ace and little Philip went to Sadie's house, it was easier that way, with the Great Aunts being there already. Glenda Faye, Josh and his friend Kevin Mc Nally, went to Mrs. Kelly's home on 16th Street. The whole family, except for the two boys who were in the Pacific, would be there.

The evening brought more snow along with a stiff wind on New Year's Eve, Maggie came in brushing snow from her shoulders and stomping her boots on a throw rug. She took off her coat, hat and scarf, she then took the baby from Ace and let him get his outer garments off. Sadie was right there to take the baby, she could not keep her hands off of the little guy. Mr. Mann had coined that phrase, "Little Guy." Maggie could smell the familiar odors coming from the kitchen, she loved ham and cabbage with big fluffy potatoes. She walked into the kitchen and gave her Great Aunts a big hug and kiss, they already had on their holiday paper hats. Maggie asked, "Could a young colleen get a cup of warm tea in this kitchen?" Immediately Aunt Rose got her a china cup and saucer with hand painted violets and green stems. She put in a metal tea ball filled with Maggie's favorite blend of tea and poured boiling water into the cup. Sadie came into the kitchen, she sat down with the other women and had a cup of tea too.

Mr. Mann and Ace went to the basement where Philip kept his home brew, he made the best beer in town. He told everyone it was a secret recipe that was passed down from generation to generation, really Philip just lucked out and found a good recipe on his own. Philip opened the basement window and took two beers from the snow outside, these should be just the right temperature.

"Wow, there is nothing like a good cold beer to settle your nerves," said Ace. The two men laughed and went upstairs with their brew in hand. Sadie told Ace there was also, homemade grape wine and Irish whiskey for a good old fashion, "Hot Toddy." Ace declined, he told her he wanted to leave room for the meal they were about to sit down to.

Maggie stood up at the table, she lifted her crystal glass of soft cider and made a toast. "Here is to my family, you have given me every blessing a woman could ask for and raised me to be the best that I can be. My gift to all of you, are my children, the one who is here and the other who is on the way. I love you all more than I can express with only words, Happy New Year to one and all." Said Maggie. Everyone responded to Maggie and raised their glasses with tears in their eyes. The meal was served in each household around Speedway City that night to welcome in baby New Year 1943.

CHAPTER 23

"BUSINESS IS BOOMING"

The new year, 1943, was celebrated with a bang and everyone had hopes for a better year to come. There was not one household that did not wish for the war to be over and done with. They wanted their boys to come home, there were way too many flags, with stars on them, hanging in windows in the town of Speedway City.

It seemed everyone was busy trying to make ends meet, John and Red had received a confidential letter from the government. John was almost afraid to open it. He thought maybe even with his injuries, that the army may recall him into service. If so, he knew he would go, but he did not want to leave Red with one child and one on the way. John held his breath, as did Red, while he broke the seal of the large envelope. The letter stated that the rationing program was going to be expanded over the next three months. Right now civilians were limited to three pairs of leather shoes per year. In March, meat would be rationed to 28 ounces per week. April would bring the largest rationing yet, it would include not only items, but Red and John would have to freeze wages for their personnel. There would be a price freeze on items and along with meat, fats, canned goods and cheese will be rationed too.

Red and John knew this news could not leak out, there would be a run on the store and good people would turn into hoarders and fight for what they wanted. John said, "I will put this envelope in the safe, you are to tell no one, not even your best friends. We will be fine, I will figure out a way to deal with everything. We cannot have or take more than our neighbors are allowed." Red did not say anything, she was shaking, she knew it was not about the news they had received, it was far greater, and it was the war. It was on their doorstep and getting closer.

That night John sat down at his desk after dinner, he had a plan, he would start ordering seeds of every kind to stock the store. He would have Maggie's Great Aunts make large posters saying, "Buy seeds, start a victory garden and can your own food for next winter. Do your part for the war effort and your families." Red was looking over John's shoulder, she thought to herself, what a great idea. Maggie's mother and father always had a huge garden that supplied all their needs except for the basics. She knew flour, sugar and spices would be hard to come by.

Glenda Faye received a call from Sadie, she was asked if she could stop by, the Great Aunts were here visiting. Glenda loved the aunts, when she pulled up she saw Red and Maggie walking into the house. Glenda covered her face against the blinding snow, it was February, and very cold. When the three girls were sitting on the couch, Aunt Rose walked out of the kitchen with a garment in her hand. "Glenda Faye, this is the first outfit we have finished, we want you to have it. If you would be so kind, please go into the bedroom and change, we cannot wait to see how you all like it." Said Aunt Rose. Glenda changed into the skirt and top, even though she was barely showing with her pregnancy, she marveled at the fabric and how fashionable the outfit was. Glenda Faye came out and did a stop and slow turn so everyone could see the garment. "Wow, said Maggie, I want one too." Red was right behind Maggie in her wish for a new outfit. The aunts had constructed the top and skirt from a fine navy blue gabardine material, there were box pleats in the front and back of the top. They trimmed the top with a white collar and cuffs and put pearl buttons down the front. The suit was tailored and stylish, there was nothing like it on the market, at least not in Speedway City.

Over tea, in Sadie's kitchen, the aunts went on to tell the girls they had hired five women seamstresses. They would be working from 8:00AM to 5:00PM Monday through Friday and Saturday would be a half day. We told the women they could really set their own hours, as long as the work was finished properly. Some will take materials home to work on, if that works well with their schedules. We were sorry to have to turn down three women, they were good seamstresses, but not perfect, we were looking for perfection to build our business on. "Business, said Maggie, I thought this was just a project for the three of us to look up to your standards." "Oh my goodness, said Aunt Rose, we have a name on the window and everything. It is called, "The Great Expectation Boutique."

Maggie, Red and Glenda Faye were meeting at the drugstore with their babies in their buggy's. The weather had taken a warm turn for February and they all wanted to get out and take some fresh air. Glenda Faye said, "I went to a meeting of the board of directors at St. Ann's to discuss the new OBGYN wing at St. Elizabeth's on Monday. No less than ten women stopped me and asked me what store I purchased my new navy blue suit from. I guess we can tell the aunts that they are a big success." Red spoke, "I have some news of my own, we quickly hired the three ladies that the aunts turned down. They are already making affordable smocks and skirts, one of the ladies came up with the idea of a jumper style. This way you can still wear your favorite blouses under the jumper. We only had ten smocks in the store on Monday, they were so cute, and I was wearing one myself. By closing time we were sold out, they loved the poka-dot, striped and floral fabrics. One lady told me it was the first smock that she would have that was not made from feed sack print. The ladies love that they can work at home and take care of their families and still make a wage to help out. We buy the material from the Great Aunts and then pay the ladies for their labor. John came up with an idea that really helped, each lady is given a packet with the material, buttons, thread and pattern, if needed, to complete a smock or skirt. It works like an assembly line, kind of like General Motors, without the grease." The three girls laughed and had their ice cream sodas and felt the sunshine coming through the plate glass window.

Sadie was taking Philip and Austin their lunch at the lumberyard, it was a fine day for a walk with March right around the corner. Sadie walked in and she was swamped by Austin and his wife Minerva, both talking at one time. Mr. Mann leaned back in his swivel chair and smiled, he thought, poor mother, get yourself out of this one.

Sadie got out of her coat and hat and sat down on a long bench by the big iron stove. She had calmed the Bates' down, now Minerva took the floor on her own. "Austin and I have come up with an idea, first mine. Do you think that the name for a bakery shop called, "The Cake & Cup," sounds nice. You know like cakes and cupcakes, the way I do them, what do you think Sadie?" "Wait a minute, what about Austin, where does he come into play here?" said Sadie. Austin moved his chewing tobacco to the other side of his mouth and spit into the sawdust container, then he stood up. "I am not much one for words, but I made this here table, now watch this. Austin turned a square table into a round table in a matter of a minute. How do you like that" Austin asked. Philip could see that Sadie was lost, knew he would have to step in and explain it all to her.

"Mother, here is how it all came together, when Minerva heard about the maternity shop, she thought she could have the aunts make her flyers advertising her cakes. She would have little cards with her information printed on them. This would be for baby showers, weddings and birthdays, just any occasion. Austin came up with an idea for this table for catering the affairs, with linen cloths supplied by the Foo's Chinese laundry. He wanted to call his table rental business, "Table For Ten." Said Philip. Now I understand thought Sadie, the Great Aunts Business had turned into four businesses already. Sadie stood up, she said "I believe you have a hit on your hands, we can put flyers in all the stores and businesses on Main Street." Minerva came flying at Sadie and hugged her, she continued on with her story about how her son, Billy, loved to bake too. She kept Sadie busy talking until the five o'clock whistle blew, and she walked home with Philip.

When Maggie heard the news from her mother about the Bates new business, she told her about Red and John too. Sadie already knew about the affordable maternity clothes at the, "One Stop Shop," there was not much that got by Sadie. Maggie leaned back and put her hands on her back, this pregnancy was different than with Philip. Her back hurt and the baby was starting to flutter like a butterfly. Sadie was holding her grandson on her lap feeding him mashed bananas, his favorite, she knew what the doctors said about how to feed a baby, but she knew her way worked well.

Ace was coming by the Mann's for supper, they tried to get together at least once a week. Ace loved to play chess and checkers with Philip, he was a crackerjack when it came to board games. Philip had a playing table that he hand made with inlaid light and dark woods and rubbed with fine oil to a brilliant shine. Sadie and Maggie had laid the table and called the men in to eat, Philip Harold was sitting in his high chair, behaving very well. These were the moments a mother puts in her heart and brings them out when she feels sad and blue. It worked for Sadie till the day she drew her last breath.

Chapter 24

"MARCH COMES IN LIKE A LION"

Red and John closed the store early due to a late winter storm, to Red, it seemed like it was just yesterday when she was strolling down Main Street in a light jacket. John was sitting in front of the fireplace playing with Patrick, Red seeing them together like that gave her an idea. She had supper ready, fried chicken, baked beans and potato salad, all of John's favorite foods. Red walked into the living room and shooed the two men in her life away, she spread out a quilt on the floor, and announced they were going to have a picnic. John started laughing, only his tiny wife would think of such an idea on a cold snowy night.

Patrick was sitting with his plate between his legs, he held his spoon in one hand and was shoving baked beans into his mouth with the other. Red had cut up some tender parts of the chicken for him, but no matter how small she made the chicken pieces, he always spit them out. The young couple laughed at the sight of their young son, he was growing by leaps and bounds. It seemed to Red that she was buying clothing and shoes every other week for Patrick. She wondered what kind of man his father had been and what he looked like? When they went out, everyone said that Patrick was the, "Spiting Image," of John. They both had soft brown curly hair, big dark brown eyes and both had olive colored skin. This made John so proud, he never for one moment thought of Patrick as not being his own son.

Red took Patrick up to the bathroom to clean him up and get on his pajamas for bed. John picked up all of the picnic mess and washed the dishes for Red, he loved doing things around the house to help her. Now that she was pregnant he worried that she was working too hard and might harm herself or the baby. He knew there was just no stopping his little dynamo of a wife, but that was just one of the things he loved about her.

Without warning, there was a faint banging on the front door, John reached for a tea towel and dried his hands as he walked to the door. When he opened the door there stood a young woman, John reached for her and she collapsed in his arms. John carried her to the living room couch and laid her down carefully and then he yelled, "Red, get down here now!" Red thought to herself, what in the world could be wrong for John to raise his voice like that to her. She laid Patrick down in his crib and handed him his favorite blanket, she placed a kiss on his forehead and turned out the light. Red made for the door and took the steps at a run, as she saw John and the person laying on the couch, she stopped dead in her tracks. John just looked up at Red and said, "Have you ever seen anything like this before, I wonder who she could be?" Red shook herself and knelt down beside the woman, she brushed her hair out of her face with a gentleness only a nurse knows how to do. Red looked at John and said, "John, I know who this is, it is Rebecca Berry, the woman who sews for us, but what has happened to her?" Red told John to call Glenda Faye and Maggie, she would need their help with this mess. The woman had been beaten beyond recognition, her legs were skinned to the bone and flaps of skin hung off of her kneecaps. When Red brushed her hair back, some fell out in her hands. She could tell that the woman had been dragged across a rough floor of some kind by her hair!

John went to make the calls, he relayed to Maggie and Glenda Faye what was taking place at their house. Both of the women said they would come immediately to help Red in any way they could. Glenda Faye went for her first aid kit and her black leather bag that contained all of her instruments for delivering babies. She had no idea what she might need? In the bag were scissors, tape, syringes, Novocain, suturing needles and thread, among other items. Glenda left to stop and pick up Maggie on her way to Red and John's home. The snow was still falling as Maggie ran out to the automobile, Maggie did not say anything, and they rode in silence to Red and John's.

When Glenda and Maggie entered the Ryan house they could see there was a lot going on. John had cleared the dining room table and placed a thick quilt and white sheet over it. He had a few pans of water boiling on the stove, Red kept giving him instructions and he followed them to the letter.

As Glenda Faye knelt down in front of the injured woman, she reached over and gave Red a hug. Glenda asked the woman what happened to her, Rebecca opened one eye as far as possible and tried to talk. The blood was pooling in her mouth, all she would say was, "No hospital and Kevin didn't mean to hurt me." Maggie spoke, "That Kevin Berry, he has always been a trouble maker, Mr. Kelly had to fire him for drinking on the job, just last week." "Don't blame Kevin, I was bad, he didn't like me sewing when he said he was the man of the house. He came home tonight and I was sewing on buttons. I should not have been doing that." Said Rebecca.

"Let us get her onto the table, we need to cut these wet clothes from her body and get her shoes off." Said Red. John picked Rebecca up as gentle as possible, but she let out a blood curdling scream, John almost dropped her, she scared everyone. There would be no more screaming, Rebecca had lost consciousness, which was a mercy for her. The girls went right to work, Glenda went into the kitchen to sterilize her suturing needles and thread among other instruments she would need. Red and Maggie undressed the poor woman, all she had on was an old faded dress and a ragged pair of underwear, and she did not even have on stockings. They washed Rebecca with hot soap and water where there were no deep wounds. Red dabbed the wounds on her face with gauze squares and hydrogen peroxide to clean out any dirt. Everything had to be kept as sterile as possible to ward off any infection that might set in later.

Glenda Faye came in with her tray laid out, she injected the woman's knees and sewed the flaps of skin in place as best she could. She then cut away some of her hair and stitched her scalp and the two lacerations on her cheeks. She would always carry these scars with her, but Glenda did the best she could to make tiny stitches to alleviate deep scarring. Glenda Faye turned to Maggie and Red, she was shaking now, "I am scared, I think we should take Rebecca to the hospital," said Glenda. Red said, "Not yet, she was emphatic about that when she came to us. Let's observe her for a few more hours and see how she progresses."

It was Midnight when Rebecca Berry opened her one eye, she looked around at everyone sitting on chairs, some dosing. It took a few minutes for her to remember what had happened to her. Kevin had lost his job at General Motors and his drinking got worse as each day went by. He was a hard person to deal with on a normal basis, but the drinking made him a mad man. She tried to hide her sewing from Kevin, he could not stand the thought of his wife making money and him being a bum. She remembered when he came through the door, he was caked with snow and then he saw her sitting there sewing on buttons. He did not break stride, he jerked her up by her hair and punched her in the face and head. He then dragged her across the wooden floor and the splinters dug into her knees. Rebecca remembered passing out two times, but Kevin threw cold water in her face. He said a lot of curse words and kept hitting her, and calling her names, until he was finally done with her. When Kevin stomped out of their little house on eleventh street, she could only think of Mr. and Mrs. Ryan, who lived on fifteenth street. She had no family or friends in Speedway City.

Maggie heard Rebecca moaning first, she jumped up and went to her, and Rebecca raised her hand and patted Maggie. She whispered, "Thank you, but don't blame Kevin, it was my fault." Maggie got raging angry, she said, "I will blame Kevin Berry, he will pay for this, he almost killed you this very night. You did nothing but try to be the best that you could be for him and this is the thanks that you get!" By this time everyone was around the table, Red placed a pillow under Rebecca's head. She opened Rebecca's mouth just a little to make sure there was no more bleeding. It was a miracle that she had not lost any teeth, there were a few that were lose, but still intact. Maggie came over and took the woman's temperature, it was normal, that was good, and no infection had yet set in. Rebecca had survived with no broken bones, she would heal physically in a few weeks, but the abuse she suffered would stay with her for the rest of her life.

John came in to check on everyone, he remained in the background to give the women privacy. He went to Rebecca and spoke sweet soothing words to her, John had a way with people, that was why he did so well at the store. John had set up the day bed in the sunroom for Rebecca, she tried to tell everyone she had to go home to Kevin or he would be angry. Red said, "There is no going back to Kevin Berry tonight or any time soon, he does not know where you are and it will stay that way!" John carried Rebecca to the day bed and laid her down on the soft mattress and covered her with one of Sadie Mann's, big comfy blankets. Rebecca took his hand and gave it a squeeze of thank you.

The girls took turns watching Rebecca through the night. When the sun came streaming through the windows, you could see the snow had stopped and already started to melt. Red was in the kitchen fixing breakfast for everyone, the other two girls had called their husbands and given them updates so they would not worry. There was a knock on the back door, Mr. Murphy opened the door and stomped the snow off his boots. Red gave him a mug of hot coffee and sat down with him. She was just getting ready to tell him about their employee, Rebecca Berry when he said, "Have you heard on the radio, they found Kevin Berry in the White River last night. He jumped from the bridge and hit a large boulder sticking out of the river bank.?" Red hung her head, she said to Mr. Murphy, "No, I had not heard of the death, but we have his wife here in the sunroom, he beat her half to death last night and she came here." Red left Mr. Murphy and called for John to sit with him. Red told Glenda Faye and Maggie the news, the three ladies went to the young woman and relayed the news about her husband. She looked up at them and said, "Now, what will I do now, I am pregnant and have no where to go?" Glenda Faye went for her stethoscope immediately, when she returned she asked for permission to examine Rebecca's abdomen. Rebecca nodded yes to her question. Glenda put the instrument in several places and asked Rebecca how far along she was? "Not sure, don't know, just been getting sick every morning for a month now." Said Rebecca. Finally Glenda found the fluttering quick heartbeat she had been listening for. "Your baby lives, thank God Kevin did not hit you in the stomach or this little one would not have lived." Said Glenda Faye.

Maggie fed Rebecca some broth through a glass straw, she was too sore to try to eat. Mrs. Murphy came into the sunroom, she went to Rebecca, and she was like the mother she never knew. Irene soothed her and hummed an old Irish lullaby until she was sound asleep. She sat with the patient while the girls went to eat breakfast. Ace and Josh both called again, they wanted to know when the girls were coming home. Glenda Faye told her friends that she had talked it over with Rebecca and she would take her to St. Elizabeth's until she delivered and was back on her feet. She could then return to her life making a living sewing for the store and others who needed the service. Mrs. Murphy would take care of her until John could take her to St. Elizabeth's later in a day or two.

Everyone said their good-byes and Rebecca thanked them all as best she knew how. This was a sad situation indeed, this poor eighteen year old girl hardly able to care for herself, now having to face raising a baby all alone. At least now she had friends to help her, "True Friends of the Heart."

CHAPTER 25

"THANK GOD FOR SPRING"

The late winter snow melted away as quickly as it had come. The sun came out and stayed out, which brought with it warm breezes. The pussy willows were in bud, the daffodils and crocuses were peeking out of the ground showing tiny purple and yellow tips.

Red and John were having a hard time explaining to customers about the ration booklets that they had received in the mail. Some of them thought they should have more than others, especially when it came to the allotment of meat. "How do you expect me to feed my family on 28 ounces of meat a week?" asked one woman. John tried to remain calm, but his nerves were at the breaking point, Red stepped up and took over. She had a stern way about herself, she explained that they were not to blame. It was the war and all meat was going to the factories to be canned and sent overseas to the troops. Mrs. Murphy came into the store with Sadie and Mary Kelly, they stood and listened to what was going on.

Sadie stepped up and told the ladies that they needed to come to the union hall meeting on Monday night. They had many ideas on how to clothe and feed a family with the rationing that was put in place. The ladies calmed down and Sadie went around and wrote down everyone's name on a sheet of paper who wanted to attend. She then told them to bring any recipes they might have that could stretch a meal for a large family. Sadie told them she still had a cookbook written during the great depression, it had many recipes that could be of use.

John thanked Sadie for saving the day, he just did not know how to handle a crowd when they were out of control. Sadie said, "John, this is just the beginning, it will get worse from here on, be prepared. Keep a lock on your meat locker and hire a night watchman." "Don't you think that is extreme?" said John. "No, I do not, I still remember how people would fight over a molding loaf of bread or half rotten meat during the depression, just think it over." Said Sadie.

Josh and Ace were busy at the airport, the loads that they were getting in from General Motors and many other factories like International Harvester were more than they could handle. They could not buy new airplanes with the war taking every scrap of rubber and metal to make their own airplanes. The two men would just have to find other transporters to help with their load. The money was good, but they were a small business and could not grow any bigger with the freeze on hiring at this point in time. Ace and Josh were sitting in the office when Glenda Faye came in carrying little Shawnee in her arms. Josh thought to himself, what a beautiful picture, she looked so pretty in her new spring outfit made by the great aunts. Her hair was pulled up on the sides and hung to her waist in the back. The light blue material made her hair shine in many different colors of red and brown. If Josh could pat himself on the back for picking Glenda for his wife he would.

"What are you two up to, laying down on the job, I thought you would be chasing your tails with so much work?" said Glenda. The boys laughed, Glenda told Ace to go to the automobile and fetch her basket, that she had brought them lunch. The three of them ate the cheese sandwiches, pickles and cake she brought with her. She told them to enjoy, because these items would soon be hard to come by. Josh was holding his daughter, she was so light in his huge arms, but she could now sit up with just a little aid. Her curly blonde hair was laying in ringlets against her scalp. He thought that he must be the luckiest man in the world.

When Glenda Faye left the airport, she went to visit with her mother. Mrs. Kelly and her two best friends were seated around the dining room table. There were stacks of different colored printed paper everywhere. Mrs. Murphy was sorting the paper into stacks of five pages and Mrs. Mann was stapling them together. Glenda Faye handed Shawnee Mary to her mother and took off her jacket. "Is there anything I can do to help," said Glenda. Glenda read some of the pages, there were wonderful recipes and helpful household hints. Mrs. Kelly had even included her recipe for making homemade soap and window cleaning product.

The women worked for two hours getting everything ready for the big meeting at the union hall. When the time arrived there were men and women in attendance. The men asked to be heard too, they were given their chance to speak. They had ideas on how to collect old rubber inner tubes and have Mr. Schmidt, the cobbler resole shoes. There were so many ideas and recipes handed in that Sadie knew they would be visiting the printer again soon. Mrs. Kelly suggested they make a spiral bound book, like they did for the St. Christopher's Festival cookbook. Everyone voted on each suggestion when they were asked to do so. All in all, the meeting went better than expected. The president of the union hall gave the women free reign for the use of the hall, except when union meetings were taking place. The thrift store and food bank were growing, everyone wanted to do their part to help their little town of Speedway City. Mrs. Mann and Mrs. Kelly sat dates to teach the women how to can everything from vegetables to juices and jams. Mrs. Kelly even knew how to can meat, this was a long process and took two secessions to complete the lesson.

Mr. and Mrs. Bates bought more live stock to provide meat for the town. They were raising chickens, pigs and cows with the stray turkey here and there. The local farmers on the outskirts of town, who were not included in the ban of raising animals in the town limits, followed Mr. Bates lead. If all went well, Speedway City would come through the war in good shape. No one would go hungry or do without the necessities to live.

John Ryan's idea of a victory garden took off, he had to order more seeds and even some newly started plants from Mr. Crawford's greenhouse. These plants would help jump start the season and the canning could get started in early August. John was so happy that everyone was excited, the children were given little paper pails with a packet of seeds when they came into the store. They would be growing bean plants in their window sills until they could take them outside to grow in the ground.

Maggie and Ace had a huge parcel of ground where their house was built. The laid out six areas and gave them to people who had no backyards or a place to grow vegetables. The condition was that they were to tend the plots and keep them well manicured and watered. Mr. Fleenor and his wife Mary owned a horse and plow, they came and turned the soil for anyone who was in need. The Fleenor's had lived in Speedway City since before it was an official city. Everyone called Paul the mayor, even though he really was not the official mayor. Nothing happened in Speedway City that the Fleenor's did not know about, they loved to gossip, but strictly in a nice way. The Fleenor's had the finest garden in the city, he always grew the first ripe tomato and won prizes at the State Fair for his crops.

The girls got together for lunch and discussed how well everyone was doing coping with a World War. Maggie said, "Keeping people busy and productive give them a purpose and we all need that in our lives." The other two girls agreed with Maggie, they knew she was level headed and right most of the time. Like when they had problems back in nursing school, she went straight to the telephone and called for help from her daddy, as she always called him. They ate their lunch and had to hurry back to their big appointment. Today was the ribbon cutting on the new renovation and new wing on St. Elizabeth's Home For Unwed Mother's. One thing that Glenda Faye did was to change the name, it was now just, St. Elizabeth's Home.

There was a huge crowd gathered at St. Elizabeth's and it was a fine spring day with warm sunshine. The newspaper reporters and the mayor were in attendance for the grand opening. There was a huge twisted pink and blue ribbon across the steps leading up to the new wing. Glenda Faye was holding the biggest pair of scissors that the Great Aunts owned to cut the ribbon. They had to wait for everyone to snap photos for the newspaper and their own personal use.

Sadie had her old Kodak on hand for the occasion, she was taking one photo after the other. Before the crowd gathered she took several photos of the three girls together, they all wore the latest maternity suits. They looked so beautiful with hats to match made by the Great Aunts. Then she took some of the girls with their families together. The outfits the girls wore were mint green, violet and pale yellow, all the colors of spring. Sadie, Irene and Mary all wore new dresses made for the special occasion. The Great Aunts were seated in the front row, they all giggled and admired their handy work. They were proud of their accomplishments.

Someone tapped the loud speaker microphone, it squealed and was then silent. Glenda Faye walked up with scissors in hand, she made a short speech, of course Glenda had to put in her two cents worth about how unwed mothers were treated. She let the crowd know how she felt and shameful was not a word that was in her vocabulary. She quickly changed the subject and asked the crowd for a count down from three to one. The ribbon was cut and the crowd was invited to come in and observe the new facility.

Everyone was in awe of the labor and delivery rooms. The nursery and a special care unit for premature babies, that St. Ann's did not even have yet. There were many rooms, with two beds to a room for the women who would be coming for care. Glenda did not cut corners, she put her inheritance to good use and hoped the McAtee's would be proud of what she had accomplished this day.

CHAPTER 26

"SPRING HAS SPRUNG"

March was winding down, the weather held and the month went marching out like a lamb. This was and old saying, "March comes in like a lion and goes out like a lamb." Or visa versa as the case may be. Maggie was walking Philip over to her mother's house on this fine spring day. They were making Easter plans, Maggie wanted to host the party this year. Maggie thought her mother had done enough over the years and needed a rest and to be a guest for a change. She had discussed it with her friends and they were in, they were going to ask some of the girls who worked for them at the store to help cater the affair. Mr. and Mrs. Bates would bring the new, "Tables for Ten," and Mrs. Bates had been saving her baking ingredients for the occasion. There had to be an Easter cake with bunnies and spring flowers made of sugar and butter cream icing.

Sadie surprised her daughter by saying, "You know Maggie, I am tired this year, I have been working so hard on the war effort. It would be nice to come to your home and just be a guest. Thank you for thinking about me and my needs, that means so much to me." Maggie had tears in her eyes as she walked around the table to hug her mother. They were sitting drinking from their favorite china tea cups with the little violets and green stems. Maggie thought as she raised her cup, if only this little cup could talk, what a story it would have to tell.

The plans were put in motion for the Easter party, Red and Glenda Faye were doing their part. The two women, now showing their pregnancies, were standing on two ladders taping up different pastel colored streamers. Josh and John walked through the door, John yelled at the women. It startled them and their ladders started to rock, the men grabbed the ladders and then their wives legs. "What do you think you are doing climbing up on a ladder in your condition," said John? "We were doing fine until you two came in here like tornados yelling at us," said Red. The men finished doing the decorating that required climbing up in high places. Glenda Faye and Red went into Maggie's kitchen and drank a Coke together. They had to laugh, it wasn't funny to the men, but to them it was.

Easter morning St. Christopher's Church was filled to overflowing, the morning was glorious. The weather was warm and sunny, everyone had on their very best suits and dresses. Maggie, Red and Glenda Faye wore the same suits that they wore to the opening of St. Elizabeth's wing. The babies all looked so sweet in their little suits and Shawnee Mary in her ruffled dress and bonnet. The three complete families, the Mann's, Murphy's and Kelly's took up almost one forth of the church. Everyone who could come home for this holiday was here, Maggie and Ace's house would be full.

The house was so festive, there was a huge cake in the center of the sideboard baked by Minerva Bates. You could smell two of Mr. Bates' smoked hams baking in the kitchen along with baked beans and macaroni and cheese. Everyone brought a covered dish of some sort, the Great Aunts did not bring any food, they were never known for their culinary arts. They supplied the paper hats and trinkets for the children. It seemed like there were so many young people running around, half the neighborhood had stopped by to wish them happy Easter. They too brought something to eat or drink. There were no formal invitations when it came to a party in Speedway City, the more the merrier.

All of the ladies were in the kitchen, Glenda Faye had sent Josh to pick up Rebecca Berry from St. Elizabeth's. Rebecca now looked so pretty, Maggie had done her hair in a side part so her hair hung lose on one side and hid her scar. Red had furnished a pretty pink striped seersucker maternity suit for her to wear to the party. "Ladies, I don't know how to thank you, I feel like a queen today with my new suit and white shoes to match. I even have on stockings with little pink ruffles around the top. You all think of everything," said Rebecca! "If there was not a war going on, you would have had silk hose instead of cotton stockings," said Maggie. All the ladies laughed and went on with their fixing of the many dishes that were brought in. The men had set up two long tables to lay out all the food on for a buffet luncheon.

As the party started to wind down, the young girls who had come to help cater the party, showed the women out of the kitchen. They informed them to go out and stay out, they were going to do all the cleaning up today. This was something totally new for everyone involved. The older women went to the side yard to watch the children at play and the men pitch horseshoes. There was a large tub filled with soda pop and, of course one in the back filled with iced cold beer for the gentlemen.

Mr. Bates stood up and cleared his throat with a loud sound, everyone looked his way. He said, "I am not much one for words, but I would like to take a moment to thank our God for bringing us all together today. Also, for keeping our Speedway City boys safe in the Pacific and other parts of the world. Neighbors we are and neighbors we will always be. Thank you all for listening to an old man's speech." Everyone who could, stood up and cheered Mr. Bates, he blushed beet red, his squat little wife came and gave him a big hug. Everyone knew it was just a matter of time till the war actually came to Speedway City and there would be a black ribbon across a flag hanging in someone's window.

Maggie was laying in bed rubbing her stomach, Ace walked in, he stood and watched her. She was humming a little tune, he couldn't put his finger on which song it was. "Great party, Maggie, you and the girls really outdid yourselves this time. Your mother had a wonderful time being able to join in with all her friends and no be stuck in the kitchen all day," said Ace. "Yes, I wanted to repay her in some way for all she and her friends have done for so many, all of these years. So many occasions, I cannot count that high, party after party, with no complaints on her part," said Maggie. Ace snuggled in close to his wife, she opened her arms to him and kissed him long and strong. Ace reached over and turned out the bedside lamp.

Mr. and Mrs. Mann were talking while they were getting ready for bed, Philip said, "Sadie, we sure raised a great daughter, she made me proud today. I can see her taking the reins one day without so much as a bobble on her part. You taught her well how to make people feel at ease and welcome in her home." "I agree with you, Philip, the three girls worked very hard on this party, just like myself, Irene and Mary used to when we were young brides and mothers. Sometimes it is like looking into a mirror of your own life, but the faces have changed," said Sadie. Philip opened the window just a crack to let the spring breeze blow in, he kissed his wife and laid down and slept peacefully.

This same scenario played out at the Wakefield's, Ryan's, Murphy's and the Kelly's houses. Everyone had enjoyed the grand Easter party and all agreed it was the best yet. That seemed to be the way they thought about their parties each year, the best yet!

CHAPTER 27

"APRIL SHOWERS BRING MAY FLOWERS'

Rain came in right after the grand Easter party, it was a steady rain that lasted for a week. Everyone gave up on umbrellas, they were just walking around in the rain. The rain was warm falling on all the flowers and plants, it seemed everyday there were more and more shoots in Sadie's garden. She was out working in the rose garden when Maggie and Philip came running up to the porch. "Hello, there, come on up and sit down, I will be there in just a minute," said Sadie. Sadie walked around to the porch and sat down in her rocker, she pulled off her gloves and then she reached for Philip Harold. She loved to hold Philip and rock him on her lap, it reminded her of her own children who had been rocked in this very chair.

Maggie stopped by to ask her mother if she had heard about the big Memorial Day party to be sponsored by General Motors? Sadie replied, "Yes, there are flyers up on the bulletin board in the union hall, I think it would be a fun day for the whole town. Everyone would bring their own food and General Motors would supply the tents, drinks and games for the children." "Well we have a month to get our group together and plan what we want to take and save our meat rations for chickens to fry," said Maggie. What would Memorial Day be without watermelon and fried chicken, the men of Speedway City would build a huge grill and put corn on the cob on it. The corn would be still in the husks, that had been soaked in salt water first. This was a delight when the shucks were pulled back, then the corn would be dipped into melted butter. The two women sat and drank iced tea and talked about what was happening in their town and with their families.

Glenda Faye was visiting Rebecca Berry at St. Elizabeth's, she had packed a gift basket for her. As Glenda walked into Rebecca's room, she was sitting looking out over the lawn. Rebecca turned around, then she got up and came over and hugged Glenda, like she had not seen her for ages. They both started to laugh, Glenda took off her light sweater and sat down on Rebecca's bed. "I brought you some goodies, I thought you might need cheering up. I know how lonely you must be, and like so many that have forgotten your circumstances, I have not", said Glenda. Rebecca took the large basket and pulled back the cover, in it lay a wonderful nightgown with a robe to match and slippers. She carefully laid these aside and then she saw several little soft baby gowns and undershirts. There were small cotton striped baby blankets for everyday use, to bundle the baby. At the bottom was a new dress and shoes, the dress was for her coming home from the hospital. Glenda had picked a sky blue dress with big white flowers, soft and flowing material, she had the shoes dyed to match the dress.

Rebecca broke down in tears, she took Glenda in her arms and cried tears of joy for this precious woman who was her friend. "I don't know how to thank you, all these gifts for my baby and the dress, oh my, I have never had such a beautiful dress. I know it is to wear home after I am discharged from the hospital, but where will I go," said Rebecca? Glenda Faye said, "I have given that a lot of thought, I know I should have talked this over with you first, but I seem to jump in and go for it. If you don't want my gift, you do not have to accept it, but here is what I am doing for you and your baby."

"I have had Mr. Mann and Mr. Bates over to your old house on the corner of 11th Street, I purchased the house, I am the owner now. These two men have been working part time building and painting the inside and out of the home. We have had a lot of time donated, since the hiring freeze was put in place, but people who know you want to help. There are pretty curtains and newly slip covered sofa and chairs in the living room. The appliance store donated a new small stove and an electric refrigerator for your kitchen. In the corner of the dining room there is a new Singer sewing machine. You can work out of your home and the bus line is only a block away from the house. What do you think, Rebecca," said Glenda?

Rebecca was speechless, this was too much to take in, how could she let Glenda and the whole town do so much for a, "Nobody like herself!" Rebecca related her thoughts to Glenda, she told her it was too much and that she did not deserve it. Glenda said, "Well then, I will just have to find another seamstress to give the house to who has a new baby. Let me see, do you know someone else that deserves to be treated with respect and love?" Rebecca hung her head, she felt like a fool, she turned to Glenda and apologies for rejecting her gift of love.

"Glenda, I want to thank you and the town for everything you have given me, I accept it all with love straight from my heart. I have to learn that people are good and I too am good. My baby will be proud of his or her mother and the baby will know you and your two best friends as Aunts. I have no real family, but now I have a whole town standing beside me. How God has blessed me, that cold snowy night, He sent me to the right place to be cared for and healed," said Rebecca.

Glenda Faye and Rebecca went for a walk around the grounds of St. Elizabeth's together, the sun was finally peaking out from behind the clouds. The two women made a bond that day and it would never be broken, Glenda new what it was like to be poor with material goods, but she was never poor in matters of the heart. Glenda kissed Rebecca good-bye and walked to her automobile, she slid behind the steering wheel, noticing that the gap between her stomach and the wheel was closing in. She smiled to herself and thought, it won't be long now.

CHAPTER 28

"MAY DAY AT ST. CHRISTOPHER'S"

Each May, there was a celebration at the church. This was the time when all the early spring flowers were in bloom. The little girls would make and wear wreaths of Lily of the Valley around their heads. All of the parishioners were dressed up for this special day. It was dedicated to the, "Virgin Mary," the mother of Christ. There was a special mass said in her honor and the alter boys would carry her statue out of the church and around the grounds, before returning her to her place of honor in the side chapel. The young children looked so special in their white dresses and the boys with white shirts and black trousers. Some of the girls were wearing their first communion dresses for the second time.

Maggie, Red and Glenda Faye sat with their squirming children on their laps during the mass. It was hard to keep them occupied, they were passed from one adult to another to calm them down. The church was hot today, even with the windows open, there was no breeze and it was very humid. Mrs. Kelly and her two friends were seated with their husbands. Mrs. Mann noticed that the paper fans in the pews no longer advertised the funeral home. Sadie had gone to the priest and told him how Mrs. Kelly felt about the fans. With the loss of her daughter, it would make it even harder this year. The fans now advertised the St. Christopher's Festival to be held on July 9th of this year.

After the mass, Sadie invited everyone over for homemade ice cream, where she got her sugar, was a secret. Mr. Bates supplied the milk and cream, his wife brought early spring strawberries to add to the mixture for freezing. Mr. Mann rolled up his shirt sleeves, held his cigar in the side of his mouth and started to fill up the two ice cream machines with ice and rock salt. He called on Ace, John and Josh for help cranking the big wooden machines. The men liked to act like this was work, but they loved to sit and drink their beer and talk about the war and current events in Speedway City.

The women were gathered on the front porch, the three girls were sitting on the steps, each one comparing their bellies. So far, Glenda Faye took the prize, she was so thin to begin with that she looked larger than Red or Maggie. The babies were down for their naps in the back bedroom, Sadie had turned on a fan to cool them for a sound sleep.

Mrs. Kelly went to their automobile and brought back a basket, she pulled back the checkered cloth and there were stacks of cookies to go with the ice cream. "How do you women do it, where do you get your sugar and spices from," asked Red? "That is our secret, but I will let you in on how I make my cookies, I sweeten them with applesauce that I put up last fall," said Mrs. Kelly. The women sat and talked about everything, the children, the war and how much they missed their brothers being gone.

Maggie asked Glenda Faye and Red, "Did you hear that, Blossom, is coming home from New York for the Memorial holiday?" They both shook their heads, no, they had not heard that news. Blossom, as they called her, was really Lotus Foo, her family ran the Chinese laundry downtown. She became a close friend of the family while the girls were still at St. Ann's School of Nursing. All of their uniforms were cleaned and starched at the Foo's place of business.

Maggie remembered when Blossom had to go to New York to attend nursing school. St. Ann's would not allow Chinese to attend their school. Blossom was a bright student and was now a resident and on her way to becoming a doctor. The youngest Foo daughter, Pearl was the flower girl at the triple wedding. "I cannot wait to see Blossom, it has been forever, I miss her smile and her sense of humor. Will the whole family be at the Memorial Day party," asked Red. "I do not know, I will call Mrs. Foo and get all the details. You all know what it is like to talk to Mother Foo, very difficult, with her accent," said Maggie.

Irene Murphy heard the first baby crying and then there were three, the ice cream was ready at the same time. The three mothers went in to change their children and bring them out. They decided an undershirt and diaper was good enough for eating cookies and ice cream. Patrick stuck his hand in the dish set in front of Red before she could stop him. He shoved a handful of strawberry ice cream in his mouth all at once. He sat very still and then he shuddered and put his hand to his forehead. "Brain Freeze," everyone said at once. They could not stop laughing, Patrick started to cry, but Red just couldn't help herself, she had to stifle her laughter.

The girls couldn't help themselves, they handed their children off to their grandmother's and challenged their husbands to a game of croquet. The older women started laughing as they watched their young daughters waddle over to the side yard. Sadie asked the other women if they thought they were a big with their pregnancies as the girls were?

The big game was on, Maggie put her foot on the back ball and hit it with all her mite. The ball didn't make good contact and rolled a few feet towards the nearest wicket. She let her Irish temper get the best of her and a frown came over her face. Her husband made it worse by laughing at her, but she couldn't stay angry for long and soon was laughing too. The girls ended up winning the game. The accolades went to Red, she loved the game and was good at it.

Everyone packed up their belongings and said their good-byes. Little Patrick was being fussy, Red felt his head, and he had a fever. She motioned for Maggie to come over and feel his head and asked her if she thought it was anything to worry about? Maggie said, "It is probably just the heat, he has been running around non stop all day. Give him a cool bath before you put him down for the night."

CHAPTER 29

"ILLNESS STRIKES THE BABIES"

The morning after the May Day celebration Red went in to get Patrick ready to go to his grandmother's. He was laying in his crib, he was awake, but listless. This was not normal, he usually was standing up shaking his crib, wanting out. He always woke up hungry, Red had his breakfast ready for him in the kitchen. Mrs. Murphy would take over and bathe him and dress him at house when Red left for the store.

Red picked up her little boy, he was burning up, and she ran for John who was reading the morning paper at the kitchen table. "John, feel Patrick's head, his whole body is hot and he has a rash all over his stomach," said Red! John took his son and did as Red asked, immediately he stood up and told Red to get ready, they were going to St. Ann's emergency unit. Red stopped long enough to call her mother and tell her about Patrick. Mrs. Murphy told her she would call Maggie and Glenda Faye.

Red was afraid it was the German measles, if this were the case it could be deadly, there was no vaccine for this disease. Thank God all three girls had been through the measles as young children. Red remembered being kept in a dark room for two weeks, the German measles effected the eyes and could cause blindness. The Ryan's wasted no time in getting to St. Ann's, by the time they arrived Dr. Anthony was waiting for them. Mrs. Murphy had called ahead and gave him the information on Patrick's condition.

John and Red carried their little boy through the swinging doors of the emergency ward. How many times, Red had passed through these doors and John thought back to the snowy night he carried his first wife into this ward. Now it was his little son, laying so still, not even crying, he thought maybe that was a good sign. He did not know that the baby was dehydrated and was producing no tears. Dr. Anthony took Patrick in his arms and asked the Ryan's to follow him to the children's ward on the third floor.

Maggie and Glenda Faye were worried, what if it were the German measles, could they have exposed their unborn babies to this dreaded disease? They took their children to their mothers houses and went to the hospital to be with Red and John. Mr. and Mrs. Murphy were sitting in the waiting room, they joined them. "Any word yet," asked Maggie? Mr. and Murphy shook their heads. Waiting was the worst, finally Red came down to fill them in, she looked worn out and pale. She gave them an update on Patrick's condition, they were running IV solution to hydrate the little boy. Red told them he was not crying, just laying there and his eyes were rolling around in his head. That was all Red could manage, she broke down and laid her head in her mother's lap. Mrs. Murphy consoled her daughter as best she could, Maggie too, was talking to Red with words of encouragement. "Let us wait until we know something for sure, before we jump to conclusions," said Maggie.

Maggie was paged from the overhead telephone, when she picked up, Sadie said that Philip was running a temperature too. She informed her that Mrs. Kelly said, little Shawnee was also, ill. "Bring them to the hospital immediately, don't wait, this may be a grave situation," said Maggie! She hung up the telephone and relayed the message to everyone in the waiting room. Maggie called Ace and Josh at the airport and told them to get to the hospital as soon as possible, all three children were sick.

The young men broke every speed limit, they got stopped by the Indianapolis police, but he let them go on to the hospital. When they walked in they were right behind Mr. and Mrs. Mann and Mr. and Mrs. Kelly. They handed the babies over to the nurses, only the parents could come upstairs. Even on the third floor there was a waiting room, the children were taken away to be examined and then the doctor would come out and let them know what was being done to aid the children. The men paced the floor while the girls sat, they were uncomfortable with their pregnancies and the room was so hot.

Red was sitting up one minute and then slumped over the next. Maggie screamed for a nurse, that was all they needed, Red could not get sick now. John was afraid all the excitement might endanger her going into labor too soon. The nurse instructed John to carry her to a stretcher and wheeled her to a room. There they bathed her with cold water and alcohol, soon she came around. "What happened, where am I, how is my little boy," said Red. "Calm down, you fainted, probably from the heat and worry, sometimes our minds just shut down," said the nurse.

Maggie and Glenda Faye went into the curtained off room where Red was laying on a bed. Red was boiling mad, she wanted up, she wanted to see her son. Maggie filled her in on what they knew, one good thing, it was not the German measles, Dr. Anthony called it, a disease that they had never heard of before. The girls were too interested in the outcome to want to know the medical name of the disease. It is easily passed from one child to another and moves fast. We will keep them here and keep them well hydrated and given medication to take care of the diarrhea that has already started with Patrick. They will be in quarantine for a few days, when the rash disappears and the fever has returned to normal you may take them home.

Maggie spoke, "Where do you think they picked up this disease?" Dr. Anthony asked if they had attended any large parties or gatherings lately? The families knew there was always a gathering of some kind or being at the store among strangers and their children. Dr. Anthony knew it started with Patrick and spread to Philip and Shawnee Mary on May day.

The girls all said they would stay with their children, but their husbands insisted they go home and rest. They could do no good, if they too got sick from exhaustion. Reluctantly the three women agreed, but the grandmothers took shifts along with the husbands so everyone could go to work.

A week later all three of the children were back home safe and sound, Patrick was eating them out of house and home. Maggie was also feeding Philip a lot of soup and he loved scrambled eggs and tiny pieces of toast, the doctor told them to give them what ever they would tolerate. They were healthy children and not one was a picky eater, except for Patrick, he did not like chicken.

Maggie, Red and Glenda Faye met at the drugstore and discussed what they had been through. They could not imagine losing one of their children, Maggie thought of her mother, losing her little son at the age of six. "Let us talk about the Memorial Day celebration, are you all ready to waddle around and have fun," said Glenda Faye? "Yes," answered Maggie and Red in unison.

CHAPTER 30

"MEMORIAL DAY CELEBRATION"

The morning broke with a blazing hot sunrise, everyone in Speedway City was up early looking forward to the celebration at the park. General Motors had set up three huge striped tents and four small cooking tents. They had donated the money to have a shelter house built with restrooms for the men and women. There was a drinking fountain located on the outside wall of the restrooms. These additions would be put to good use today, the park was located in the back lot across from St. Christopher's Church. There were plans for the city to put up swings, slides and other equipment for children to play on.

Mr. Mann and Mr. Bates left at 4:00AM, they and some others were putting two large hogs on spits. The would take turns rotating the hogs and basting them with a concoction that Minerva Bates had sent for this purpose. Of course after the men ate their picnic breakfast and the fire got low, they broke out the ice cold brew. They took their time drinking, it would be a long day and neither of the men liked the feeling of being drunk. Also, they had wives that would have skinned them alive for abiding with too much libation.

Maggie and Ace were getting everything ready, she had the chicken fried and the potato salad made. The baked beans were in the oven and would be taken out just before they left for the party. Little Philip was sitting in his highchair playing with some cornflakes that Maggie sprinkled on his tray. Ace came up from the basement carrying their folding table, he would make two more trips to get everything they needed for the picnic.

Glenda Faye and Josh were repeating the same scenario in their house, except Glenda had made a big bowl of ham salad and a lovely fresh fruit salad. Shawnee Mary was laying in her port-a-crib playing with toys hanging on the handles. They would be taking the crib with them, she was still too little to climb out of it. Glenda also knew there would be a play pen there for Patrick Joseph and she could put them together to play.

Red and John had ordered all the products needed by General Motors for the picnic. There was a large trailer full of straw and big blocks of ice. He and Mr. Bates had delivered two horse watering troughs to the park the day before to load with blocks of ice, rock salt and water for the bottled sodas. One smaller trough would be used to ice down all of the bottled beer and homemade wine. Most people were Irish and even the ones who weren't liked a cold beer on a hot day in May.

Sadie and her friends were driving over together, they were heading up the ladies league and had a lot of preparation to take care of. The men of the town donated some of their gasoline rations so there could be a small Ferris wheel and a ride that had many swings hanging from chains. The swing ride was their favorite, when it got going really fast the swings were practically straight out in midair. Without the gas donation, there could be no rides. There were many men riding their bicycles and walking to work for a month, to make so many children happy.

Mr. Kelly and Mr. Murphy were in charge of soaking the corn on the cob. They had their charcoal grills burnt down to a low flame that was ready to receive the ears of corn. They had melted a small amount of butter with lard to make it stretch further. Here again, the ladies had donated their butter and Mr. Bates had furnished the fat rendering from his hogs. After the corn was salted, you could not tell there was any lard in the mixture. Glenda Faye new about this secret and it took her back to her days as a student at St. Ann's. She was on a charity scholarship and she had to eat in the kitchen. The cooks made her a sandwich smeared with lard, instead of butter. The girls still laugh about, "The famous lard sandwich."

The men parked the automobiles at the far end of the park, they let the families out first and then parked the cars for them. This was so nice not to have to drag so many things a long way. The minute the children got out of the automobiles they were off and running. General Motors had all kinds of games organized for them and for the adults too. There was a raffle for a new automobile, and many small household items. Every child received a prize of some sort, little dolls for the girls and toy boats and cars for the boys. There were even baby rattles and round rings of many colors for the babies. General Motors did it up right this year of 1943, there was a saying that, "Speedway City was the town that General Motors built."

The Murphy's, Kelly's, Mann's, etc. all found each other and the boys set up an open sided tent for their family. Mr. Bates brought two of his, "Tables for Ten." This family was growing so quickly, along with strangers that became friends, like Rebecca Berry. She was there too, she was wearing a cool green smock with light tan slacks. These were a gift from the Great Aunts. Yes, of course they were in attendance too, without their paper hats this time. The aunts were laughing when children ran by blowing paper whistles.

John set up the playpen for Patrick and the girls put all three children in together. Shawnee was having a hard time staying upright, the other two older children kept knocking her over. She burst into tears, Glenda Faye picked her up and gave her a cool bottle of weak apple juice. The other two boys got along famously. They shared their toys and when no one was looking, they laid down and went to sleep.

There was so much food on the tables, the women and men went and brought back plates of roast pork and corn on the cob. Everyone ate while the babies were sleeping. There were quite a few young teenage boys cranking ice cream machines under one of the big striped tents. Here again went their sugar rations for a month, but this party was worth the sacrifice. Mr. Mann could taste the ice cream on his wife's apple cobbler, just thinking about it made his mouth water. No one made an apple cobbler like Sadie Mann, she would pass this recipe down for many generations to come.

While the men played horseshoes, the teenagers played lawn tennis and croquet. Women did what women do, they sat and gossiped and did needle work or held their children and grandchildren. It was a time when you did not need to be entertained or cry about being bored.

The sun was starting to set in the evening sky, when all of a sudden there was a huge bang! Fireworks, everyone stopped what they were doing and looked to the sky. General Motors planned this as a big surprise for everyone, it was just like the 4th of July, only better. With the whole town together to enjoy the show.

After the fireworks were over, everyone started to gather up their belongings and packing their baskets and boxes. The young men went to the parking lot to pick up the automobiles. They loaded what they could in their automobiles. Sleeping babies rested on their mothers chests as they rode home with smiles on their faces. It was a great day to remember for a long time to come. The men would come back tomorrow and break everything down with the help of General Motors employees.

CHAPTER 31

"PRIZES, PRIZES, PRIZES"

After the big Memorial Day party, everyone was waiting for the Speedway Press to print the winners of the raffle and prize drawing. Everyone held onto their ticket stubs until the paper was delivered on Wednesday. Mr. Murphy was always the first one up in the morning, he was an old farm boy and always got up around 5:00AM. He was sitting out on the porch drinking a mug of steaming coffee when the boy came by on his bicycle. He threw Mr. Murphy a Speedway Press right at the top step.

Mr. Murphy had forgotten about the drawing announcements, but when he saw who had won the new automobile he went running in the house. He went upstairs and woke up his wife, she shook her head and asked him what had happened? "Mother, guess who won the new automobile, never mind, you would never guess in a million years. It was Rebecca Berry, and I bought the raffle ticket for her. She did not have two dollars, so it was my treat for her," said Mr. Murphy.

Mrs. Murphy put on her robe and slippers, she went downstairs and fixed breakfast. She was waiting for a decent hour to call the girls and tell them the news. At 8:00AM, she could wait no longer, she called Glenda Faye first, since she was close to Rebecca. "Hello, Glenda answered the telephone with a sleepy voice." Mrs. Murphy relayed the wonderful news to Glenda, immediately Glenda was wide awake and laughing and smiling at the same time. Glenda said, "Let me call Maggie and Red, they will be so happy, remember when the Kelly's won the station wagon at the festival one year,"?

Everyone in the town was happy for Rebecca, she wanted to give the automobile to Mr. Murphy because he had given her the winning ticket. He would not hear of it, he had a perfectly good automobile and a truck. Mrs. Kelly won a new toaster and Sadie won a new set of cookware made of stainless steel. Mrs. Murphy won a set of glasses with the General Motors logo printed on them. The list of prizes was long, it seemed almost everyone won a little something. The children all won a ticket to the Speedway Theatre.

The Memorial Day party was a huge success, but the men in Speedway City, were disappointed again this year. There disappointment was due to, the Indianapolis 500 Mile Race, being cancelled again. All of the rubber and gasoline was going towards the war effort. Normally, people came into Speedway from all parts of the United States and even some from overseas. Not only was the race cancelled, but there was no transportation to and from Europe during this time. Everyone missed the Mid-Way celebration with all the mechanical rides, the cotton candy and popped corn with caramel sauce. The night before the big race was always great fun, everyone parked their cars down Main Street and some even slept in them. This way they could be first into the infield of the race track where they laid out blankets and had their picnic lunches. This was an all day affair and most people came dragging home with bad sunburns.

June started with hot weather, but then a cool spell came in and brought with it nice warm showers. All of the victory gardens were flourishing, there would be a bumper crop this year. Sadie and the other women that met at the union hall were having meetings devoted to learning how to can foods properly. There was an art to canning, if you did not do it right, your food would spoil and you might end up with food poisoning. The canning lessons were packed every Tuesday, Sadie and Mary Kelly were in charge. They went down a list of vegetables from tomatoes, which included many products. There were whole tomatoes, ketchup, tomato juice and chili sauce, this was Sadie's own recipe.

Maggie, Red and Glenda Faye were not working, they were in their last month of pregnancy. Poor little Red looked like an egg with skinny arms and legs. Maggie was doing well with her weight, as was Glenda Faye, her height helped her to keep her shape more than her other two friends. The girls were at Mrs. Kelly's house rolling bandages and boxing them to be sent overseas. They could not just sit and read magazines and eat chocolate bon bons, like so many women did when they were eight months pregnant. Sadie was holding Philip and he was having a big time unrolling the bandages that she gave him to play with. He would unroll it and she would roll it up again.

Ace and Josh were working from dawn to dusk at the airport, with the hiring freeze on, they each had to do the work of two men. Ace was sitting at the desk when Josh came in and sat down. "What are you thinking so hard about," asked Josh? Ace replied, "I was thinking about our wives, they are so pregnant, Maggie looks like she might burst at any minute. What amazes me is none of them complain and I know they must be so uncomfortable." Josh agreed with Ace, he too knew that Glenda Faye was having a hard time, he rubbed her back every night to give her some relief. Caring for a six month baby and carrying a new one could not be easy. "I have an idea, why don't we have a surprise party for them, we can have it catered and eat on our summer porch," said Josh. Ace said, "Count me in, I will talk to John and their mother's."

CHAPTER 32

"A NIGHT TO REMEMBER"

It was not easy trying to fool their wives, but with the help of Mrs. Mann and her two best friends, the boys pulled it off. Or at least this is what they thought would happen. Sadie sent invitations to the girls for a baby shower to be held at Glenda Faye's house the night of June 10, 1943. Sadie asked Glenda for permission because her own home was so small and there would be a big crowd.

The day of the shower Mrs. Kelly asked Glenda Faye to go shopping with her to downtown Indianapolis. She said, "You dress up and look pretty, we will stop at one of those little booths and have our picture taken together." Glenda Faye thought she should stay home and see to the plans for the shower. Her mother assured her that Sadie and Irene could handle all of the arrangements.

Maggie and Red were together, they had dropped their children off at their grandparents homes. The grandpa's were in charge, all three were together at the Murphy house. The grandmothers would sneak home later and take over the babysitting. Glenda Faye left Shawnee to spend the night or she thought, with her father and younger sister, Beverly.

The three girls arrived together, they got out of their automobiles. Red said, "Now, we have to act surprised, that is what my mother said to me." The other two girls said they would follow her lead. The house looked dark from the outside, but there was a small amount of light on the summer porch. When Glenda Faye opened her front door, she and the other two girls could hear soft music playing. There were candles burning and bouquets of flowers everywhere. Maggie whispered, "What in the devil is going on here, where are all of the people?" "I don't know, your guess is as good as mine," said Red. The girls looked down and there was a trail of rose petals leading through the house.

The girls stepped softly down the trail of flowers, then all at once their husbands stepped out of the darkness. The girls jumped, it scared them, but they now had an idea of what was going on. The three men had on their best suits and ties, the offered their arms to their wives. The men escorted the women to the summer porch, a big round table was laid out with the finest linen and china. There was a silver bucket with sparkling cider and another with fine wine for the men.

Then the men softly said, "Surprise." The girls had tears in their eyes, they were truly surprised. Ace pulled a chair out for Maggie to sit down and the others followed his lead. Josh said, "Tonight is your night ladies, we want you pampered and to feel the love we have for you. We may not always show you the attention we should, but tonight we hope you will feel loved and cherished." Now the tears were streaming down the faces of the three girls, they were handed a handkerchief from their husbands.

Mrs. Minerva Bates had catered the supper, there was a platter of fresh vegetables cut in fancy ways with a dipping sauce. For the main dish there was a chicken salad with walnuts and raisins on a bed of lettuce and fresh yeast rolls. For dessert, she had made a berry cobbler with home made ice cream. It was a perfect summer dinner for the six of them to enjoy and remember.

Josh got up along with John, they walked into the other room and came back carrying three baskets. Each basket was tied up with different colored cellophane and a bow. The baskets contained Minerva's peppermint lotion, a large sea sponge, lemon scented soap and a gift certificate to Flo's Beauty Shop. The girls all looked at each other in amazement, how could these rough and tumble guys come up with this wonderful idea. They figured their mother's played a large part in the preparations.

The night was perfect, there was dancing and toasting mixed in with laughter and tears. Glenda Faye stood up and toasted the three men, she said, "Here is to three of the most wonderful men on the planet. Thank God they belong to us, we must count our blessings this night and every night to come." Maggie and Red thought to themselves, there is no way to top that toast. They both agreed with Glenda and said so by raising their glasses of sparkling cider to their husbands.

The three couples said goodnight to one another and went to pick up their children. When they got home each one of the girls received a back and foot massage from their husband. They were tucked into bed and kissed goodnight. Maggie laid awake for a while, she could not believe how grand the evening had been. She only wished she wasn't so long into her pregnancy, she wanted to make love to her husband. Not only Maggie was having this same thought, Red and Glenda Faye were snuggled up to their husbands too.

The next morning each girl went to see their mother's, they all scolded them for keeping the secret. Each mother asked, "Well, did you have a fine time, are you sorry for being surprised?" The answer was no all around with the three girls. Maggie and Sadie were having iced tea on the front porch while Sadie watered her flowers. She had a way of doing this in the front of the house so she could sit in her rocker and sprinkle in every direction. Maggie loved the American Beauty climbing roses on one side and the Honeysuckle on the other. It closed the porch in and kept it cool, the scent was breathtaking.

Glenda Faye and her mother were visiting Mrs. Murphy, she was showing off her fancy needle work. There were so many perfect little sweater sets in shades of blue, pink, yellow and mint green. Mrs. Murphy was not taking any chances with the babies being born female or male. She had it covered, with all the colors of the rainbow. Mrs. Kelly only wished she was good at needle work like Irene. She just never had time to learn, raising eight children and taking in laundry. Maybe now, she could learn to knit or crochet, she preferred crocheting, the stitches were easily ripped out to start over. If you dropped a stitch in knitting you were in big trouble.

Red and John were at the store, Red was sitting in the big swivel rocking chair in the office. She had her legs propped up on the stool beside the desk. Her feet were swollen today, she felt so heavy and bloated. Taking care of a baby already born by someone else was a snap, compared to carrying one for nine months. John came in and handed Red an ice cold Coke from the new machine he had just installed. You put your nickel in the machine and then you opened a long door and pulled your Coke out of a hole. What a great invention this was, no big tubs of ice to mess with.

Beverly and Paul were busy stocking shelves, they were working full time now that school was out. John put part-time hours on their time cards, but paid them under the table for full time work. There was always a way to get around the hiring and hourly wage freeze. The kids were good workers, Beverly loved working in the dry goods section, but John needed her at the cash register most of the time. Standing all day was for a young person, he had the older women in the other two sections. Red got up and picked Patrick up from his playpen and put him in his stroller. She was going to walk home and enjoy the pleasant weather they were having.

Red walked by all the stores that lined Main Street, she thought back to when she and her two best friends would walk together and go in search of boys. Arm in arm, skipping down from one drugstore to the other, she could just see herself trying to skip now. Red laughed out loud, Patrick Joseph, turned around and started laughing too, but not knowing why. As Red walked she felt an aching in her back, her baby was laying low now. Dr. Lucas Anthony said it could come anytime around July 1st. They were not sure of her actual date of delivery.

CHAPTER 33

"THE SUMMER BLUES"

June was winding down, but the cool weather remained, that was just fine with the three pregnant women. They were all at Mrs. Mann's house today for a real baby shower this time. No surprises, just a lot of friends with so many presents. There were buggies, strollers, playpens and so many baby clothes. Glenda was glad for all of the diapers she had been given, as were Red and Maggie. Red was trying to get Patrick potty trained before the baby came, but she was having no luck.

Mrs. Kelly told Red to bring Patrick over for a week and she would have him trained in no time at all. Red thought about it, but could not leave her son with someone for that length of time. Mrs. Kelly gave her another choice, "When you are in the hospital having your baby, I will train Patrick, you will have to leave him with someone. Who do you know that has done more potty training than me," said Mrs. Kelly? Red agreed, Mrs. Murphy said she would be stopping by to see Patrick everyday and she would not have that to worry about. This was a load off of Red's mind, could these women possibly get the job done?

Maggie was talking to Mrs. VanCamp, she and her husband had been in Florida at their winter home for five months. This was so nice to have her back, she was all tanned and beautiful. Her blonde hair was perfect, but it was always perfect. She had on a pale blue dress with peek toe pumps and a matching floppy brimmed hat. Mrs. VanCamp looked like a movie star in one of Maggie's Photoplay magazines. Maggie told her she wanted this baby out, not in a bad way, but she was just about at the end of her last nerve. Having to deal with Philip and all the bending and lifting was getting to her. Philip was pulling up and trying to take steps around the furniture, but he would not be walking when the baby came. Mrs. VanCamp offered to have a nanny sent over for the first few weeks after Maggie delivered. Maggie told her that she would wait and see how things went when the time came.

Glenda Faye didn't seem to be as bothered by her pregnancy as her two friends. The case being, Glenda did not complain, she had been having some contractions on and off for the past two weeks. She did not tell anyone except her mother. Dr. Jacob Adam said they were probably just false labor pains, it happens with the first baby more than with the second. Glenda's due date was around the 15th of July, she still had two weeks to go. She knew from working in the maternity ward that a woman could go two weeks early or two weeks late. There was no perfect way of telling your due date, unless you knew for sure the very night of conception.

Beverly Kelly was making a bouquet out of all the ribbon bows, and Paul was picking up all the wrapping paper for Sadie. She had invited Paul, she knew he would have a good time and loved to be with his mother and big sisters. Sadie served some of Mrs. Kelly's magic applesauce cookies and lemonade. There was also tea and coffee for those who wanted a hot beverage. Sadie had saved her rations for the baby shower, she wanted it to be perfect for the girls.

Sadie looked over on the table at a photograph of the three girls taken on their graduation from nursing school. They were all lined up like soldiers with their white starched aprons and caps on. On the opposite side of the frame was a photograph of them on their wedding day. They looked so pretty, Sadie had to laugh a little at Red. Her hair was just starting to grow out from being a Sister of Charity at the time. She looked like a little pixie, but she was beautiful in her full fairytale dress.

Where does the time go, the years were passing Sadie by so fast, there was so much going on all at once. Her one son was now fighting in the Pacific and the other working long hours at International Harvester. The boys had no children yet, but she was sure when the war was over, there would be more grandchildren on their part.

Ace, Josh and John came to pick up their wives and all of their loot, it was a man word. The automobiles were piled to the roof and the trunks were tied down with rope in one case. Glenda Faye had received another playpen and a stroller, they were sticking out of the trunk. The men could tell that their wives were happy, but very tired. As they drove home each girl played the day over in her head, what a great day it had been.

Mrs. Mann knew how to throw a party on a shoe string budget, she had done herself proud. Mr. Mann sat on the porch with Sadie, he reached over and patted her hand and said, "You did well today mother, and the girls had a wonderful party."

CHAPTER 34

"GLENDA FAYE HAS THE BLUES"

Glenda Faye was awake on and off all night, the cramping in her abdomen came and went. She decided that a call to Dr. Jacob Adam would be in order if this condition did not let up by morning. As Glenda laid there she thought about Rebecca Berry, a month ago when she was visiting her, they were sitting on the new veranda talking. Dr. Jacob Adam walked up to them and said, "How are you two beautiful ladies this fine summer morning,"? Rebecca replied, "You work with those quick stepping pretty nurses, and you call me beautiful. I have this swollen belly and scars on my face, now that is not beautiful." Jacob raised his voice to Rebecca, she was startled and gave a small jump. He turned to her and said, "Don't you ever let me hear you say anything like that again. Yes, there are pretty girls at the hospital, but they do not have the internal beauty that a man is looking for in a woman. You, Rebecca, are beautiful outside and inside, to me you shine, and that is all that matters." Jacob turned and walked away, you could tell that he was angry.

Rebecca was in tears, she came to Glenda for comfort. Glenda told Rebecca that she thought that Dr. Adams had a sweet spot in his heart for her. "Do you really think so, what does he see in me, that I do not see in myself," said Rebecca? "I am positive, Glenda told Rebecca, the next visit with him, be your own sweet self. Apologize to him for being rude and get to know him, give him a hint that you care about him. If you have no feelings for him, let him know that too," said Glenda. "Oh, but I do have feelings for Dr. Adam, every time he is here I get the shivers and I am tongue tied. My words come out the wrong way. You saw that for yourself just a few minutes ago. I will try to make this up to him, now that I know how he feels," said Rebecca.

Glenda smiled to herself laying there in the dark, her plan had worked, and Jacob and Rebecca were falling in love. They were both morbidly shy, but there were times when Jacob would hold her hand or put his arm around her. Rebecca had talked to Jacob about the situation and let him know that he was not to play with Rebecca's heart. He let her know in no uncertain terms that he was in love with Rebecca and planned to ask her to marry him. He had already discussed the situation with his parents in New York. His mother was old fashion, but she just wanted happiness for her son. Glenda told Jacob that he had better hurry the process along, Rebecca was due to deliver in September. They both laughed and he assured her that Rebecca would have a ring on her left hand before the end of the month. Jacob kept his word, Rebecca now sported a beautiful Tiffany set solitaire diamond ring.

The couple decided to stay in the house in Speedway City that Glenda had given to Rebecca, he still had his residency to be completed. Rebecca loved being so close to Glenda and her two friends. They would make a home and family together just as she and Josh had.

Glenda drifted off to sleep thinking of her friends and planning a small wedding in her back yard for Rebecca and Jacob. Glenda felt Josh get out of bed, but she stayed and waited for the next cramp to come. Sure enough, the cramp gripped her and then in about ten minutes another cramp came. She did not get up until Josh went downstairs. Glenda swung her legs from the bed to the floor, she put on her slippers and stood up. A cramp doubled her over, but it did not last long. She called the doctor's service to see who was on call, it was Dr. Adam. She dialed St. Elizabeth's where he was working today, she was connected to his telephone by an overhead paging system.

Dr. Adam told her to come to St. Elizabeth's for a good check over, she was two weeks early according to their calculations. Glenda put her long hair in a shower cap and then turned on the cool water. She brushed her teeth and stepped into the shower, the water felt good as she soaped her body. She patted her belly and said, "It won't be long now my little one, we will meet face to face, and I love you."

Josh was pouring coffee into a large mug when he saw Glenda come down the stairway with her hospital bag in hand. He spilled his coffee and almost dumped the whole pot all over the stove. Glenda set her bag down and came to her husband, she took the mug from his hand and gave him a towel to dry off his hands. "Sit down, have your coffee, we have plenty of time. I have already spoken to Dr. Adam, he will be waiting for us at St. Elizabeth's," said Glenda. "I am so glad that you, Maggie and Red decided to have your babies at the new hospital wing delivery unit. It is state of the art and with our baby being early, there will be staff there to look after that problem too. Hopefully, there will be no problems, but I feel good about Dr. Adam and the staff at St. Elizabeth's," said Josh.

Glenda looked at her husband and said, "I guess we will be having a new babe this day, my Joshua." Josh loved it when Glenda spoke to him in a thick Irish brogue and called him Joshua. Josh jumped up and went to the telephone, he was going to call Mrs. Kelly, but Glenda stopped him. She wanted to wait, to be sure, before they called anyone. Josh started laughing and dialed the telephone, there was no waiting for an event like this. Mrs. Kelly answered the telephone and Josh told her the situation. Mrs. Kelly said she would make all of the other telephone calls for them, their job was to get to the hospital as soon as possible.

When Glenda Faye and Josh arrived at the hospital Dr. Adam had one of the nurses there waiting with a wheelchair. Glenda tried to protest, but the nurse insisted on wheeling her into the hospital. Rebecca Berry was standing there with Dr. Adam to greet the couple ready to have a new addition to their family.

Glenda Faye was laying on the examination table when Dr. Adam came back in with the head nurse. This made Glenda nervous, what could be wrong to have Sister Clara in attendance. Sister Clara came over and did her own examination, she had delivered too many babies to count in her days as a mid-wife nurse. Sister Clara looked Glenda Faye straight in the eye and said, "Not today my dear, you are not quite there yet, you are having false labor. I know it is painful and frightening, but it will pass, go home and put your feet up and wait." She patted Glenda's hand, turned and walked out to tell Josh the news, he was pacing the floor with all of the family and friends.

Sister Clara clapped her hands to get everyone's attention, "Mr. Wakefield, there will be no baby today, your wife is having false labor. You may take her home as soon as she is dressed," said Sister Clara. There was a sigh of disappointment all around the waiting room. Glenda Faye walked out with her head hung low, she was so embarrassed, but Maggie stepped up and started clapping her hands and everyone joined in. Glenda Faye started to laugh, she knew everyone was behind her and they were there to support her, baby or no baby today.

CHAPTER 35

"JULY FIREWORKS"

The heat was stifling as Mr. Mann and Austin Bates worked with Mr. Kelly setting up tables for the 4th of July party. The cool air had moved north and the southern breeze brought with it heat and humidity to Speedway City. The men were used to the weather, they had been raised without any kind of cooling systems, except for electric fans. The Kelly's were hosting the party this year, their backyard had huge oak and maple trees for shade. No matter the weather there always seemed to be a breeze blowing across this part of the town. The Kelly house sat on the edge of Speedway City, but they were starting to build a new community, with smaller homes in the surrounding area.

Sadie, Irene and Mary were busy in the kitchen preparing all of the food to be served today. They wanted to keep the menu light, because of the heat wave they were dealing with. There would be lots of salads and of course one of the only hot items, was fried chicken. What would the 4th of July be without fried chicken? The three women decided to keep the party small this year, their daughter's were all feeling tired with their pregnancies.

Mr. and Mrs. Bates were there with their son and the two sets of in-laws would be attending too. The three women loved the Wakefield's and the Van Camp's, they fit right in with the other families.

Maggie, Red and Glenda Faye arrived with their husbands and small children. The girls handed off the children to their father's and went to the kitchen. Sadie took one look at the girls and sighed, she could tell that they had just about all they could handle. All of the girls had on pretty starched sleeveless smocks and light weight cotton skirts, but you could see the perspiration running down their necks. Glenda Faye had her hair pulled up into a high bun with a little ring of silk flowers around it. Maggie and Red had their hair pinned up too, the heat was just too much for them.

Irene told the girls to sit down and put their feet up and handed each one of them a tall glass of iced tea. Maggie said, "I don't remember being this miserable when I carried Philip Harold, I am huge with this baby." "Huge, you do not know what huge is," said Red. She was so tiny, only five feet tall, and she really was huge. Glenda Faye was worried about her redheaded friend, she hoped she could deliver a large baby without having a Caesarian section. Glenda said to herself, "Stop it, and don't think about that, you are just over thinking everything these days." Her thinking was probably due to the false start to her own pregnancy.

Everyone pampered the girls today, they would not let them lift a hand to help in any way. Their husbands cared for the children and the in-laws helped in any way they could. The tables were set with so many dishes of baked beans, corn on the cob, macaroni salad, potato salad and fried chicken. There would be cake and ice cream for dessert, Minerva made sure to have strawberry short cake, it was everyone's favorite for the 4th of July. The girls didn't eat a hardy meal, the just did not feel well, Maggie said, "At least I can go to the kitchen and cut up the watermelon, why don't you two go sit in the shade,"? Maggie headed for the kitchen, Glenda Faye went to play a game of croquet and Red was running after Patrick and playing ball with him.

Maggie was slicing the watermelon, it felt good in her hands. She had just lifted it out of a small tub of ice in the kitchen. Sadie didn't like Maggie being on her own and slicing all of the watermelon, it was a big job for so many people. Just as Sadie walked into the kitchen she saw her daughter standing there, butcher knife in hand looking surprised. Sadie looked down and Maggie was standing in a puddle of water. "I believe you need some help in here, let me wipe up that melted ice," said Sadie. "Mother, it is not melted ice, my water just broke," said Maggie! Both women were flustered, but Sadie took matters in hand, she sat Maggie down and went to announce to the group what was going on in the kitchen.

Sadie got to the door and she could see Glenda Faye, she was bent double holding on to her croquet mallet. Josh was kneeling down talking to her, she was shaking her head in agreement to what he was saying. As Sadie walked towards the crowd she saw Mrs. Murphy fixing a cold towel to put on Red's forehead. Red was wiping a small trickle of pink fluid off of her legs, John was running to his wife's side.

Sadie clapped her hands and yelled over the crowd, "I believe we are bringing in the 4th of July with a bang, bang and bang." Everyone was going in different directions, Mr. Mann stood up and calmly started giving directions that made sense. He suggested the three girls and their husbands travel to the hospital in one automobile. Sadie would call St. Elizabeth's and give them a heads up and to expect three deliveries today.

Doctor Anthony and Dr. Adam had made prior arrangements to be in town until the end of July. They knew these women would be delivering around the same time. Little did they know what was in store for them today. Sister Clara answered the telephone when Sadie called, she had to calm her down to get the message straight. "You mean all three are in labor and on their way immediately," said Sister Clara? "Yes, all three, two of the girls have broken waters, but the third one is just in hard labor," said Sadie. Sister Clara hung up the telephone and made contact with both doctors, Dr. Adam was with Rebecca celebrating the holiday at St. Elizabeth's. Dr. Anthony was at his home hosting his own holiday party.

There were three nurses with wheelchairs waiting at the entrance of the hospital. Josh, John and Ace helped their wives out of the automobile and into the wheelchairs. Maggie and Glenda Faye were moaning softly, but Glenda Faye was racked with excruciating pain and she let out a scream. Josh jerked when his wife screamed, he thought to himself, what have I done, I didn't count on so much pain. I have to pray and leave this to God, it was His plan, and Glenda Faye thought she could not have children. He came back to himself and kept pushing the chair through the hospital. Each husband pushed their wife, they would not let the nurses do it.

They arrived at the labor and delivery section of the hospital, Sister Clara met them there. She held up her hand and said, "This is as far as you young men go, and it is off to the father's waiting room for you three." Each man kissed and hugged their respective wife. The girls tried to care if they were kissed or not, but they were in too much pain to care one way or the other. They waved good-bye to the men, they were standing there like forlorn sheep ready for the slaughter.

Glenda reached for Maggie's hand and Maggie reached for Red's hand, they rolled to the labor room together. Nothing changed in their lives, they were born together, grew up together, married together and now they were giving birth together. The three girls must have been thinking the same thing, they began to laugh until another pain gripped them.

CHAPTER 36

"LABOR DAY COMES EARLY"

The nurses helped the three mother's to be out of their clothes and into cotton hospital gowns. Red had to laugh when she saw Maggie bend over to pick up her shoes. "Maggie, remember the gowns are open all the way down the back and that is not your best side right now," said Red. Maggie replied, "I could care less if I am naked or clothed, I just want this over and done, I remember now how much pain I had with Philip Harold. This is ten times worse, I feel like my insides are coming out on this floor," said Maggie!

The girls were lined up in three hospital beds side by side, the nurses were making them as comfortable as possible. Glenda Faye let out another scream and her water broke, gushing all over the clean dry bed. She tried to say she was sorry to the nurses, but they hushed her and soothed her. Glenda's bed was changed as was her gown, the nurses knew just how to do this without removing the patient from the bed.

Both doctors walked into the labor room at he same time, they were wearing surgical gowns and hats. They pulled the curtains around each woman as they examined her, when they got to Glenda Faye, they called for Sister Clara. "I believe we better take this one to the delivery room, her baby is crowning," said Dr. Anthony. Glenda Faye was wheeled off and separated from her two friends, she was scared, but in too much pain to give it much thought.

Glenda Faye was put on the delivery table and her legs were fastened to the metal stirrups. When her contractions hit, she was told to push from her back down. Glenda thought she was being ripped in half, just when she thought she couldn't take it any longer, she felt her baby slip out. She laid back and took a deep breath, she whispered, "What is it, is it a boy or girl?" "You have a big healthy boy, do you have a name for this little gentleman yet," said Dr. Anthony? "Yes, he is to be called Charles Joshua Wakefield, after his father," replied Glenda Faye. The nurse wrapped the baby in a soft striped blanket and handed him to his mother for a quick bonding. He would be cleaned, weighed and measured while Glenda was being cleaned up herself. Glenda gently stroked little Charlie's cheek with her finger, I love you already, and I have loved you for the past nine months. The baby closed his eyes and slept on his mother's breast. Glenda offered up a prayer to her God, His plan worked out well, she had her own baby, and Josh would be so pleased.

Dr. Adam was with Red, he was having her push, and she had a big baby to deliver. He still had not ruled out a surgical birth for his patient, she was so small. Jacob was nervous, Dr. Anthony was delivering Glenda Faye and this could turn ugly really quick. Red was pushing with all of her might when a contraction gripped her and then she would lay back and breathe. Maggie looked over at her little friend, she was a real trooper, and she did not scream or moan like so many women did. Maggie was having her own contractions to deal with, all she could think of was, where was Dr. Anthony, she would need him. As if reading Maggie's mind, Sister Clara, stood beside Maggie and told her not to worry. Sister

Clara assured her that she could handle almost anything when it came to birthing a baby.

Red was sitting up on her elbows, she was pushing with all of her might, Dr. Adam checked her again, and found it was too late for the delivery room. This baby was coming and coming quick, he asked the nurse for some Novocain and numbed Red so that he could cut her, the baby was just too big. Dr. Adam did not want Red to tear like so many women did, the pain would be too great to endure. Maggie was too interested in the birth of Red's baby to feel her own contractions. The did not pull the curtain and Maggie got to watch Red give birth to her baby.

"Now, with the next contraction, you push like your life depended on it," said Dr. Adam. Red was more than ready to have this baby delivered, she felt the contraction start and she started pushing too. "It is coming, keep pushing, push harder one more time," said Dr. Adam. Red didn't think she had one more push to give, but she tried her best. "You can stop pushing this baby is out, there was a cry immediately, the baby was glad to be born. It had been quite a task for both the mother and the baby. Dr. Adam told Red that she had a big baby girl, he guessed she weighed at least 8 ½ lbs. Red laid back, she was exhausted, Maggie blew her a kiss and a thumbs up, but she was busy with her own pushing.

Red named her baby girl, Susan Irene Ryan, the nurse brought the baby to her, before she cleaned her up, weighed and measured her. "Hey, Maggie, look, look what I did, can you believe it," said Red? Maggie looked over at her friend and smiled, Red held the baby up for Maggie to get a good look at her.

Dr. Anthony came into the labor room, he was surprised to see another healthy baby laying in her mother's arms. He informed the two girls that their friend had a baby boy and named him, "Charlie." Both girls were crying, they were so happy for Glenda Faye, having her very own baby. She would, as they say, "Be over the moon," with happiness." "Now young lady, let me take a look at you, how are things progressing, are you comfortable, do you need a whiff of gas to ease your pains," asked Dr. Anthony?

Maggie replied, "No, I think I am doing fine, this is my second baby you know."

Dr. Anthony and Dr. Adams agreed Maggie had a way to go yet, they went out to see the father's and relay the news of the two births and the one still pending. Josh and John were beside themselves and started handing out the box of cigars that Mr. Mann had brought along to celebrate. Ace was still pacing, he was worried about Maggie, and she should have been first to deliver. She had already had one child, he did not know that every birth was different.

Red was being cleaned up as was her child, they would all be taken to the same hospital ward when Maggie's baby was delivered. This was the way they wanted it, the nurses thought they were all so cute. If only they knew how close these three girls were to each other and how they worried about one another.

Maggie was pushing, the sweat was pouring off of her, she reached down between her legs and could feel her baby's head crowning. "I need a doctor here, quick, the baby is coming," yelled Maggie. Sister Clara checked Maggie, she was surprised by what she saw and went running for one of the doctors. They were still chatting with the families, Sister Clara came bursting through the door, and she was yelling for a doctor.

Dr. Anthony ran into the labor room, put on a fresh gown and gloves, he went to Maggie's bed. Now it was Red's turn to watch Maggie deliver her baby. One of the nurses wheeled Glenda Faye back to the labor room, she was just in time for the birth. The doctor sat down on a little stool and told Maggie to give it a big push, the baby was out to the shoulders, he told her to push one more time. Little, Saragene VanCamp, came sliding out into the doctor's hands. Maggie laid back, just as all mothers do after pushing that one last push. The doctor said, "You too, have a healthy baby girl, she is wide awake, but I cannot get her to cry yet," said Dr. Anthony. Maggie did not know yet, but her baby would hardly every cry, she would just eat and sleep. The nurse handed Maggie her baby and asked her for a name, Maggie replied, "Saragene, she will be named after my mother and my father-in-law."

Now all three girls were in tears, they were holding their babies, each one saying how beautiful they were to each other. "Maybe we can wait a while, before we populate the world with any more children," joked Red. The girls all agreed with this statement, they just wanted to see their husbands and their families.

After everyone was cleaned and the babies were weighed and measured, the mothers were wheeled to the ward to receive visitors. The doctor made his last trip to the waiting room, he announced that little, Saragene VanCamp, was now a member of this very large family. Mother and daughter doing quite nicely. Sadie and Eugene VanCamp were crying, they had no idea that Maggie was going to name her baby after them. Ace said, "Don't feel lonely, she never told me either!"

When the girls brushed their hair and washed their faces, the nurses gave them the pretty gowns they had brought with them. Maggie whispered something to one of the nurses, she walked over to Maggie's bag and brought back two pink ribbons and one blue satin ribbon. Each of the girls tied up their hair with the appropriate colored ribbon and sat back with their babies to await their visitors.

CHAPTER 37

"VISITING TIME ARRIVED"

As all the visitors were filing out to go see Maggie, Red and Glenda Faye and their new arrivals, Mr. Mann was still holding the cigar box. He noticed one of the janitors picking up a cigar butt and saying to his friend, "What I wouldn't give to have a brand new cigar like this one. These are premium brand cigars, but so expensive." Mr. Mann went over and took one cigar out of the box and tucked it into his shirt pocket and then he handed the rest of the box to the janitors. They were astonished by this act of kindness and thanked him over and over. Mrs. Mann held his hand up and told them they were welcome to join his celebration today. He became a grandfather three times today. One man said, "Triplets, that is a record for St. Elizabeth's!" "No, said Mr. Mann, my daughter and her two best friends, who are like daughters to me all had their babies within the last three hours." He then left to go see his new granddaughter, Saragene and the other babies who would grow up with her.

Sadie had her Kodak camera with her and was already snapping photos when Mr. Mann came into the ward. In a normal hospital setting, only two people were allowed in at a time. Since Glenda Faye bought and paid for this wing, she ruled the roost and her word was gold. The girls were tired, but too excited to sleep, they loved showing off their new children. Sadie was holding little Saragene, she had tears streaming down her cheeks. "Mother, you should be happy today, not sad," said Maggie. "Oh, but I am so happy that my joy is over flowing and my body cannot contain it," said Sadie. Maggie was pleased that she had named her little girl after her mother, they would all call her by her full name. When she was in school, everyone would call her, "Sara," but she would change that back in her later years.

Ace, John and Josh were beside themselves, Josh was holding his son, he was proud as a peacock. John was afraid to hold Susan, even though Red told him that she would not break. Finally he could resist no longer and Red slipped baby Susan into his big hands. She was a chubby little cupid, her lips were bowed and rosy and her hair was bright red. She had her mother's bright green eyes, John was glad she looked like Red, because Patrick looked just like him. Ace was handed his little girl, he couldn't help but let the tears run down his cheeks, and she was Maggie all over. When Saragene grew up she would look just like her mother, dark brown hair and big hazel eyes with green flecks.

Finally the nurses insisted that the family had to leave and let the girls get their rest. Maggie had talked it over with Red and Glenda Faye and they decided to stay the full ten days. Mainly this was due to having children at home to take care of and Red's stitches had to heal. It was all she could do to sit up, but she did not complain about the pain. The nurses wheeled the beds back in place and pulled the curtains around each patient. They wanted the mothers to have some private time with their new babies. When the nurses came to pick up the babies, the mother's were starting to dose off. They quietly took the sleeping infants to the nursery to be fed and changed. The babies could start learning to nurse from their mother's tomorrow, they had a hard day today and would probably sleep most of the time tonight.

On the way home the conversation in each automobile was probably the same. How beautiful the little infants were and their mothers looked so pretty with their pink and blue ribbons. Mr. and Mrs. Mann took the Great Aunts home before going to pick up little Philip. The children were being watched over by Beverly and Mrs. Bates so the families could all go to the hospital. The Great Aunts, as everyone called them, were really now, great, great, great aunts. The older Kelly sisters loved their family and they never thought those many years ago back in Ireland, that this day would ever come.

As the days passed the girls were getting bored, they had many visitors and Rebecca was there everyday. She helped them up and walked with them to the new bathroom facilities so they could shower. This was unheard of in 1943, you stayed in bed and were given sponge baths. The girls were thankful for the showers and the clean rooms. There were beds in the ward that had never been slept in yet. Only today, did another young girl deliver her baby and she was moved to the far end of the ward. Maggie would not hear of this, she told the nurse to move her bed up close so they could get to know her. Glenda wanted to speak with her and find out what she intended to do with her baby. Glenda could give her advice, when she knew her history.

Thank God for small favors, the hot weather had finally broken, the windows let in a cool breeze and sleeping was pleasant for the girls. They were counting the day till they could go home. Red knew it was up to her and how she was healing. She had Dr. Anthony examine her, because her stitches were beginning to pull and needed to be taken out. He agreed with Red and removed the stitches, he gave her a stern talking to about sex with her husband. He told all of the girls to wait at least six to eight weeks to be loving with their husbands. You could tell he was embarrassed with this part of his orders for the women to follow.

After he left the three girls were nursing the babies, they were laughing at the doctor and how red faced he became. You would think in his line of work, nothing would bother him. It should bother us, after all there was not a part of their bodies that he had not seen. They were going home tomorrow, they had their clothes laid out, and they all brought loose hanging dresses. They did not want anything tight around their waist just yet. It would take a little time to get back in shape, but believe it or not, Red was the one with the most flat stomach. She had no fat on her, it had been all baby. Now she would soon be her tiny little self again in no time at all.

Ace, John and Josh arrived early to pick up their wives, they could not wait to get them home. Their mother's would be staying with them for a few weeks to help with the bigger children and do the cooking and cleaning. The girls tried to protest, but the women loved their daughters and wanted to spend the time bonding with the new babies. Mrs. Kelly loved infants, maybe that was why she had so many children. Now she had two to take care of, which was no problem for her at all. Mrs. Murphy was so happy to have a little girl to knit for, she would make her little bonnets with ruffles around her face.

When each woman walked into her house, there was soft music and a big bouquet of fresh cut flowers. They knew Minerva Bates had been there, she had left a cake on the kitchen table and fresh brewed tea in the refrigerator. "Wasn't that nice commented their husbands." Everyone loved Minerva, she was a woman who just knew what you needed and provided it for you, if she was able.

Being home seemed strange, Maggie, sat down in the big overstuffed chair in the parlor and held her daughter. Pretty soon Mrs. Mann brought Philip over to see his new little sister, he wasn't interested. He just wanted up on his mother's lap, he had missed her so much and didn't understand where she was. Red was so glad to see Patrick and he tried to jump up on her, but she told him he had to take it gentle. He calmed down and climbed up beside her and his new little sister, Susan. He patted her head and held her fingers in his small hand. Glenda Faye had no problem, Shawnee Mary was too little to wonder what had happened or that her mother had been gone for almost two weeks. She was really a grandmother's girl, the two of them were as they say, "Thick as Thieves." She wasn't the least bit interested in her new baby brother, Charlie.

Everything settled down for the next week or so, there was a routine to life and you learned to cope with what came along. Soon the girls were planning a triple christening. It would be held at St. Christopher's Church when the children were one month old. The summer was flying by, it seemed everyday there was something different the year of 1943.

CHAPTER 38

"BEAUTIFUL BABIES"

Glenda Faye was holding little Charlie when the doorbell rang, "I will answer the door, you stay where you are," said Nanny. Glenda had taken her mother-in-law up on her offer to provide a nanny for her two children. It was just too much for her with Shawnee Mary being 8 months old. Nanny led Rebecca Berry and Jacob Adam to the sun porch, where Glenda was seated.

"What a surprise, what are you two doing out here in Speedway City, said Glenda? Jacob spoke, "Sorry for not calling, but we were at Rebecca's house checking to see how the remodel was coming along. We have something to tell you, we appreciate your offer to host our wedding in your garden, but we have to decline." "Why, it would be so beautiful and I love doing it for the two of you," said Glenda? Rebecca said, "Jacob's family want us to come to New York before the baby comes and hold a big wedding for us. I feel that their acceptance of my situation is a big act of love and I want to do this for Jacob."

Glenda understood where they were coming from, she admired the young couple for overcoming all of the problems in their relationship. Rebecca told Glenda that they would stay until the baptism, we would not miss that for the world. Glenda thought to herself, it will be a big deal, with a huge party afterward to celebrate the dedication of their babies to God. The three women had picked one of their friends to be God Parents to their own child. Red would be Godmother to Charlie, she would be Godmother to Susan and Maggie wanted her mother and father to be God Parents to little Saragene. It all worked out well, everyone was happy to stand up with the three couples on this holy day of baptism.

Jacob and Rebecca told Glenda that when they returned from New York that she would stay at St. Elizabeth's and Jacob would continue living at the resident doctor's dormitory. Jacob hadn't intended to stay on in Indianapolis after his residency, he only came to study with Dr. Lucas Anthony, because he was the best in his field. Now that Jacob was marrying Rebecca, he could not take her away from all of her friends that were now family.

Jacob and Rebecca were adding on another bedroom and enlarging the bathroom in the little house. They were thinking of the future family they might have together. It was easier to do the remodel, now, while they had the time and it would be ready by the first of September. Rebecca was due to deliver sometime in the middle of September, the young couple was so happy together. Glenda Faye sat rocking Charlie and thinking back to when she and Josh had met on the beach in Ohio, she could see that kind of love in Jacob and Rebecca's eyes today.

Sadie was at Maggie's home helping get the children ready for the baptism today. The baby, Saragene, looked like a baby doll in the christening dress that her mother had worn before her. This dress was made by the Great Aunts many years ago, but Maggie wanted her children to both be christened in it. Philip Harold wore it eleven months ago and now Saragene was wearing it. This would be repeated with Maggie's wedding dress, Sadie would one day make a first communion dress for little Saragene out of it. Little did either lady know, but Saragene's granddaughter, Bailey

Ann, would wear the little white communion dress when she was eight years old in 1998.

All of the other grandmother's were helping their daughter's prepare for the christening. The daddy's were taking charge of the other little children and keeping them occupied and out of trouble. Red knew this was a big event, just like everything else she and her friends had done or accomplished, they would be doing it together. "Mother, said Red, isn't this baptismal gown exquisite?" "The Great Aunts out did themselves with all of the ribbon, lace and ruffles," said Irene. "I love it, Susan looks like a cherub in an old fashion painting in the museum downtown," said Red. Mrs. Murphy had fallen in love with baby Susan the moment she held her. She loved Patrick, but there is a bond between female children and their grandmother's. She felt this bond grown stronger every time she held her little granddaughter.

Mrs. Kelly wanted Charlie to wear the same christening gown her children had worn, but it was in tatters. Glenda Faye felt bad about this when Shawnee was to be christened. There was just no saving the little gown when they opened the white box and looked inside. Mrs. Kelly had gone to the Great Aunts with Glenda Faye to have Shawnee Mary's gown made. They told them to bring the old christening gown with them, they did not understand why, but did as they were told. The Great Aunts took three panels from the old gown and incorporated them into the new gown. Mrs. Kelly had cried when they held up the new gown for her to see, she recognized the embroidery on the gown. "Now, now, the Great Aunts had said, it was no trouble at all, but it did turn out well, if we do say so ourselves." Glenda and her mother had relayed the story of the gown to everyone, it was agreed that the Great Aunts were angels in disguise.

St. Christopher's Church was packed with people this Sunday in August. It was decided that they would have the baptisms before the mass. This way the babies would not be tired and hungry. It made for a better service, Father Linderman told them of many tragedies at the baptismal fount in the past.

When the crowd was seated, the three couples walked down the aisle, the mothers were each holding their own baby. They were followed by Mr. and Mrs. Mann. It reminded the couples of their wedding, when the brides walked down the aisle and they were joined together as man and wife.

The three women stood elbow to elbow around the baptismal fount, the husbands stood behind them, with Mr. and Mrs. Mann in the rear. Father Linderman performed all the rituals of baptism, only one baby let out a small cry when the holy water was dripped over Charlie's head. Father Linderman asked the God Parents all of the questions about caring for these children in the case their parents could not. The God Parents were to see to a Catholic upbringing and schooling. Everyone answered the questions with a firm, "Yes."

The ceremony ended and the priest announced that the babies were now all children of the risen Christ. Everyone was silent until the three young mother's said, "We are now the sisters of St. Elizabeth's, True Friends of the Heart." Their husbands joined hands and raised their arms to make a circle around their wives, and said, "We are now brothers and also are, True Friends of the Heart."

CHAPTER 39

"SPRING 2010"

The sun was rising when Lariann opened her eyes to the new day. She laid there calm under the weight of her mother's big comfy blanket. She missed her mother every moment of everyday. Saragene, was her best friend, they were more like sisters than mother and daughter. In these quite moments, she missed her the most, because until Lariann's eyes opened, her mother was still there with her.

Finally, Lariann, swung her legs over the edge of the bed and slipped into her house shoes. She stood up and pulled on her fluffy old robe, her mother had given her this robe for Christmas before she passed away. It was a comfort to Lariann, she would wear it until the time came to pack it away with her treasures.

Lariann shuffled off to the kitchen, she stopped and turned up the thermostat. She did not want any of the three older women to get a chill, when they got up. Lariann put the old dented tea kettle on to boil and set out the three little china cups with the hand painted violets and green stems. She then took down a large mug and filled it with water and placed it in the microwave oven. She loved instant coffee with lots of cream and sugar. She only drank tea with her

Grammie Maggie, because she knew Maggie liked to share that tradition with her.

As Lariann thought back over the last week, she smiled, the three older women in her life were treasures. She had to laugh to herself when she remembered the look on Grammie Maggie's face as Red and Glenda Faye had walked into her kitchen. They were girls again their faces seemed to grow young before Lariann's eyes. They joined hands and danced around in a circle, as best they could, it was a tradition since they were children. There was so much laughter and stories. Oh, the stories Lariann had heard this past week. She had taped every conversation, except what they talked about while they all three laid in the same bed together every night that week. The ticking of the old wooden clock on the other side of the wall lulled them off to slumber. The clock had belonged to Maggie's mother, Sadie had paid a nickel a week to the newspaper who was selling the clocks at the time.

Lariann and Patti Cay had surprised the ladies with Saragene's book and the little white communion dress. Most important was the third china tea cup that Lariann gave to Maggie to make a set of three. She and her mother, Saragene, had searched many thrift stores and antique shops to find the little fragile cup and saucer.

Maggie, Red and Glenda Faye sat out on the porch with their shawls on, just like they had when they were young girls. Sadie Mann's front porch, Lariann had the fencing repaired and roses planted on one side and honeysuckle on the other. This week the honeysuckle was starting to bloom and the scent was sweet. Almost as sweet as the three ladies who would sit on the porch and tell their stories. The sad stories about the loss of their parents, some children and their husbands. These were stories that Lariann had never heard before and was glad for her tape recorder.

Lariann did not know if she was the writer that her mother was. She only hoped she could do the, "girls," justice in her own writing of their lives together. She looked at the clock on the old stove and thought the women should be scooting into the kitchen at any moment. She waited a few minutes before she went to wake them.

Patti Cay was coming over for a visit and then they were all going to the airport to see Glenda Faye and Red off. They had made arrangements for someone to accompany the two women on their flights home. They were still strong women for their age, they would all turn 91 years old in May. Lariann got up and turned the tea kettle down and went to wake the ladies from their slumber. They had a late night sitting up talking on their last full day together.

Lariann peeked into the room, she walked over and pulled up the roller shade. The sunlight streamed through the window onto the three faces of Red, Glenda Faye and Grammie Maggie. They were so peaceful, Lariann did not want to wake them up. Lariann said, "Come on you, "True Friends of the Heart," time to get up. There was no stirring from the bed, the three older women were laying with their hands interlocked. Lariann felt the tears stinging her eyes as she walked over to the bed.

This was the longest walk that Lariann had ever made, she lifted Red's tiny arm, and it was cool to the touch and had no pulse. Lariann laid her arm down carefully, she repeated this action two more times. Now Lariann slid down the wall and she sat on the floor, she was racked with sobs that tore at her very soul. The, "girls," were together forever, they did it their way, and no one could ever separate them, even in death.

Finally, Lariann managed to get up, she placed a kiss on each one of their foreheads. When it came time to kiss Grammie Maggie, she let the tears fall on her face. Grammie Maggie could take the tears with her to heaven. Lariann could not bring herself to pull the crisp cotton sheet over their faces. She left them there joined together, three into one, as it had always been. She walked over and pulled the shade down again, and walked to the bedroom door. Lariann, turned and said, "Good-bye True Friends of My Heart."

Saragene Stamm Adkins enjoyed writing the second book in this series. All of her friends, fans and family wanted more stories of the adventures of Maggie, Red and Glenda Faye.

Saragene lives near Speedway City, where she grew up. Her two daughters Patricia and Lariann still live in Speedway City, Indiana.

Saragene is still writing and painting for her friends and family and sends her love and blessings to everyone.

Saragene Stamm Adkins
sarageneann@comcast.net